The
Last Motel
for 99 Miles

KAY D

JOHNSON

Johnson, Kay D
The Last Motel for 99 Miles

ISBN 978-0-9958942-5-9 (pbk.)
ISBN 978-0-9958942-6-6 (ebook)

ONE

Gabriel had been driving through the pouring rain for hours, putting miles between him and the two goons who wanted him dead. Driving at high speeds, he didn't have much time to react, nearly ditching the car twice when the trees seemed to swallow up the muddy road ahead of him. In between swipes of the blade, he could see clearly, then within seconds, his headlights and the heavy rain crystalized his view. His knuckles hurt from gripping the steering wheel so tight, holding the car straight in the slick mud. He had started out on a paved highway that afternoon, but the further north he escaped, the more rural the roadways became. The last sixty or so miles had turned to a narrow two-lane dirt road, filled with potholes and broken branches from the raging storm above. He was running for his life, making him push himself and the old car as hard as they could both travel.

With no head lights in his rear-view mirror, he knew he could slow down some. He would have to keep moving, stopping was not an option. More importantly, the lack of lights meant they hadn't found him — not yet. It was temporary, he was sure of that, but it gave him some extra time to plan his next step, rather than racing at full speed to get away. He needed to put as much space between him and the car chasing him down as possible. The dirt road beneath the tires turned to asphalt, telling him he must be nearing a civilized area of Northern Ontario.

When Gabriel saw the street lights in the distance, he eased his grip on the steering wheel, allowing his shoulders to relax from their held tension. Driving crazy in the rain, in the dark, was not his favorite thing to do. And knowing they could show up at any moment, added to the urgency of his escape. A quick check of his wrist told him it was almost midnight. He could push it further, gaining another hour or two before stopping, hiding in the cover of darkness to grab a few hours' sleep. The further away from those two thugs, the better for him. Gravel shoulders turned to curbed roadways giving Gabriel faint white lines to visually follow through the heavy rain. An oddly placed street light here and there, illuminated his route. Much better than driving in the total darkness, going down roads that he wasn't even sure would be there until he made it to the corner.

Being near midnight, the nine-street village was asleep. Needing to connect with the major highway that ran dead west, he drove down the empty main street, making his way to the opposite side of town. A large spear of lightning flashed across the street in front of him, lighting up the alleyways headed in the street light's shadow. No humans. Not even a stray cat wanted to be out in the hostile storm. Strong claps of thunder could be heard in the distance, telling him the worst of the storm was yet to come and that meant more driving in the blinding rain. Reaching the furthest edge, he saw the words he did not want to see. Gabriel stopped the car and through the wipes of the windshield blade, he read the neon sign aloud, "The last motel for ninety-nine miles." He flipped on the interior light to check his fuel gauge. A quarter tank — definitely not enough gas to push him through the next one-hundred. Being honest with himself, he also did not have the physical energy to drive another twenty-five, let alone a hundred or more miles, in the rain-saturated darkness.

The motel sign also read 'VACANCY' in glowing white neon letters. That one word brought great relief to his overwrought mind and body. He popped the car in gear and headed for the only lit up building behind the towering sign. He had no credit cards on him but he had the funds to pay for the room in cash. No more using 'plastic' to pay for things. That's how they found him — again.

~

He thought he had lost them in Blind River. When his gut instincts told him they were ahead, waiting to ambush him in town, he took the upper less used roads around Blind River, avoiding them, gaining an extra forty-five-minute lead. It was then he understood they had traced his location through his debit card. They must have had someone on the inside, watching for any transactions on his account. One phone call could tell the two goons where he was and at what time. It was the only explanation as to how they knew he would be going that direction. After that insight, he had stopped in Sault Ste Marie to empty his bank account. It was a risky move. They could have someone watching the bank or someone on the inside, ready to make the call. But he was out of money to pay for gas, food, and the occasional motel room. It was imperative that he destroy the debit card and only use untraceable cash from then on. It took time to convince the bank teller to empty his account completely, finally agreeing and giving him all his money in an envelope. But when he saw the two thugs sitting outside the bank, he knew why it was really taking the teller so long. Gabriel ran to his car and made it look like he was headed towards the border. Regrettably, he had to leave his passport behind when he first fled for his life, so crossing into the States was not an option. Instead, he turned down a side street and hid his car amongst the others in a mall parking lot. He waited until he was sure they would be gone. Gabriel had decided on the Soo, hoping that the men hunting him down would think he went stateside, getting out of not only Ontario, maybe out of Canada altogether.

No such luck.

They were almost on his tail by the time he hit Wawa. He thought he saw them in his rear-view mirror and drove down the Main Street, making it look like he was going to take the main highway out of town. But he managed to double back, hiding nervously amongst the tourists. After an hour, he believed they were gone. He headed the other direction to throw them off again, veered north, instead of following the Trans-Canada westward as he pretended to. Unlike his normal temperament, he had turned cunning and calculating to survive. They were relentless, dogging him every day for the last four months. He would no sooner think he was safe, free of them, then they would show up, banging on doors. Or worse, as he had seen once climbing out a window — kicking in the door, guns pointed ready to kill him on the spot. Up until then, he had been able to evade their grasp, slipping out just in time. After so many weeks of near misses, he was worried his luck was about to run out.

~

He pulled his car into the last space, furthest away from the square of light falling from the office window. He hoped to them it looked like an employee's car parked for their shift. Turning off the motor, he sat quiet for a few moments, gathering his thoughts as to what he was going to tell the person booking his room. What lie would he tell this time to hide his identity in case they came snooping around looking for him? He pondered if he even needed to lie this time. The two men hadn't followed him there, of that, he was sure. There had only been one set of head lights behind him in the last three hours and they turned off long ago, heading westward down a road he hadn't seen through his rainy windshield.

He decided on half-lie, half-truth. He grabbed his lone backpack and whipped the car door open, slamming it equally as fast before running full out for the office door. The wind whipped rain into his face, stinging any flesh that wasn't covered by clothing. Just inside the office door, he shook water droplets off his jean jacket so it didn't soak through. Having to leave on the fly had taught him to be prepared at all times, and damp clothing was not an option if he wanted to stay healthy.

The lights were dimmed and there was no one at the front desk, only a silver bell with a tiny sign 'RING FOR SERVICE' taped to it, sitting in the middle of the counter. Gabriel was actually relieved since it gave him time to get himself together, to get his mind straight on his cover story. A concocted tale he was about to spin in case they came looking for him, asking for him by his real name and maybe where he was from or where he was going to. Even though Gabriel was sure they wouldn't find him tonight, he wanted to cover his tracks for future peace of mind.

All set on the details of his lie, he dinged the bell with his index finger, careful not to ring it too loud, sounding aggressive, maybe putting the clerk off. The last thing he wanted to have happen, was to have the clerk turn him away. He truly couldn't stomach another hundred-mile drive in the dark, in the rain, with not enough gas. When no one came, he dinged it again, this time a little harder. He waited patiently but no one came. With his flat hand, he hit the bell harder, producing a still pleasant-sounding ding. After another lengthy wait, he hammered the bell with his palm. Dinging it several times, producing enough racket to wake the dead. Apparently, that's what he needed to do to have the clerk come to him.

The door behind the counter opened, revealing a very drowsy man, "Yah, yah. Hold your horses." Wiping the sleep from his eyes, he pulled the bell out of Gabriel's reach, "You didn't need to ring it so damned hard."

Gabriel held his snarky comment, not wanting to start an argument over something that couldn't be changed. It was best to keep this man on his side — a gullible ally that could unknowingly save his life. "Yah, sorry about that." He said no more, keeping his words few and direct. "I'd like a room."

The man looked at him, examining Gabriel's face that was partly hidden by the bill of his baseball cap. "Double or single?" He yawned widely, sending a cloud of bad breath Gabriel's way.

Not having showered in two days himself, Gabriel couldn't even smell it. "A double."

The clerk looked him up and down, seeming to be unimpressed by the man standing in front of him. "Just the one night?" A spike of lightning lit up the windows, casting a blue light throughout the office.

"We'll see." When he was given a dirty look, he added, "I'm just winging it. If I like the town, I'll stick around for a few more."

That answer seemed to please the man. "That's great. And which credit card will that be on?"

"Um, none. Don't believe in them. Don't believe in paying someone to use my own money." He stuck his hand in his pocket and pulled out a tight roll of bills, "I prefer to pay cash."

The man's eyes grew greedily at the wad of money, "But I'll have to charge you extra. For security deposit ... in case you mess up the room."

Gabriel laughed at his words, "No chance of that happening. Right now, I'm going to jump in the shower and jump into bed." That's where he started on his list of lies. Lies that painted him as someone he wasn't. "Been on the road for a non-stop business trip. All I want to do is sleep."

Again, the man looked him over, deciding whether to trust the traveler or not. Besides his unkempt appearance and disheveled clothes, Gabriel was also missing something else. He pointed at Gabriel's shoulder, "Just the backpack? No cases?"

"Yep. The rest is in the car." Another lie. There wasn't anything more. Everything else had been left behind in Sarnia when the two men were kicking in his motel door. "I've got all I need for tonight."

"Ooookay." He pulled up the register, laying it in front of him, "Name?" Thunder rumbled to the north.

"Gabriel." He was so exhausted his real name came out of his mouth before he could stop himself. 'Shit' he swore in his head. He had wanted to use another name, hiding his true identity from the clerk and from the goons if they ever came this way looking for him. No point in correcting his mistake, that would only make him look guilty. "Gabriel Smith."

"Smith?" He picked up the pen, "That's original." Gabriel didn't react. "Don't suppose you have an address that I could enter in here." When Gabriel didn't speak up right away, the clerk tossed his pen on the desk and asked him straight out. "Look, I get you're running from something. All I want to know is … is that something gonna come here and bust up my motel."

He smiled widely at him, "What's your name?"

"Gord."

"Gord, I'm not looking for trouble. Just a place to sleep. And if it's a good sleep, I'll stay another couple of nights."

He noted the Gabriel hadn't answered his question. Thinking he was right and he was running, he'd help him lighten his load by taking most of the money off his hands. "I don't normally do this but with it storming so bad, I don't feel right turning you out." He filled out what he could and frowned at Gabriel, "Since we've agreed on a surcharge, rather than a credit card number, your total will be seventy dollars.

Gabriel nearly balked at the steep price. Even for Northern Ontario in 1988, that was a dramatically inflated fee. Yet he knew he had no choice but to pay the extortionist's price. It was twice the regular prices he had been paying throughout his four months on the road. "That's fine." He smiled, "I write it off as a business expense anyway. I'll get the receipt tomorrow, right?" He flipped over the stack of bills and began counting out tens.

"Sure thing." Gord took the stack of bills and shoved them in a box on the desk behind the counter. He turned to get the key, "Check out time is 11 AM. Extra towels and pillows are in the dresser drawers." He held it out to Gabriel with a firm warning, "Just so you know, if trouble does come, I WILL call the police. I have my regular people to protect. So, I'm suggesting you get yourself to hell out of here before whoever it is, shows up. That way, no one gets in trouble with the law."

Gabriel nodded, the peak of his cap flashing a shadow on his eyes, agreeing he understood. He coolly took the key from him, "I'll do my best." He nodded again, showing his appreciation for letting the rule slide, "Thank you."

"Room 13. No one else will take it. Thirteen being bad luck and all," he said it with a broken laugh, recognizing the absurdity of it all.

Gabriel's stomach tightened. More for Gord's crazy laugh than the number 13. "Makes no difference to me. As long as I can shower and sleep. That's all I care about right now." He turned to leave but stopped himself, "Any good places to order take out?"

Again, Gord scoffed, "Not this time of night. In the morning, call the number taped to the mirror. They'll set you up with whatever you want." He pulled the cash box from off the desk, holding it under his arm. "There's a number for booze delivery too. Just in case ..."

"Thanks." Gabriel left the office, leaving his car parked where it was in the shadows.

Through the rear picture window of the office, he watched Gord walk to the back of the tiny desk. Although he couldn't see him actually do it, Gabriel was sure that's where he hid the cash box. 'Better than under the counter,' he thought, waiting beneath the eaves overhang. Another flash of lightning lit up the center of the motel's property. It was a 'U' shaped layout with a center courtyard. Two parking spaces in front of each room. Through another flash, he saw that each room had a plastic tub chair sitting beside a narrow brick wall that separated the room's imaginary patio. One three-foot wide wall on each side for privacy. The rain didn't look like it was about to ease up so he sprinted for the overhang of the motel's roof that covered the sidewalk that ran down the front of them. His jacket pulled tight with one hand, he hurried along the front sidewalk, reading numbers on the door.

13. The lightning flashed bright over them, making the two metal numbers seem more ominous than just being unlucky. He untangled the keys from his cold fingers and attempted to get it in the slot. Between his tired fingers and blurry eyes, it took him three tries to finally get it in. He pushed the door open and listened for goons. It had become habit over the past four months. Always waiting for them to catch up with him. Hearing nothing inside, he slid his hand along the wall, searching for the light switch. Click! The instant brightness hurt his eyes. He squinted to visually scan the room, walking straight to the bathroom, searching through it for unwanted company. No one.

The tension between his shoulder blades relaxed. He took a few seconds to shake off his fight-or-flight mindset, letting out a restrained breath. He walked back to the door and locked it, using the cheap chain lock as an added warning device. Its weak metal chain would never keep Rene and Cash out. But the noise of it stopping them before they kicked the wooden door in, would give him enough time to be ready for them. He tossed his backpack on the desktop, avoiding the worn bedspread that appeared to be from its original retro period. Various shades of avocado green made up the mod floral pattern right out of the 70's. The curtains matched as well as the carpet, it being swirls of avocado coloring. He didn't want to know what lurked in that ancient carpet, he just wanted to shower and sleep — forever.

The bathroom was done in blues, mostly navy to offset the outdated turquoise toilet bowl and sink. The window was inside the tub. Small, yet big enough that he could climb through it if the goons showed up. Towels thick and fresh laundry white. He closed the door behind him and locked it. Again, that lock wouldn't stop them, but it would let Gabriel know he was about to get shot at. He carefully checked the floor for bugs. Cockroaches, ants, millipedes — they all disgusted him. It was safe to let his dirty clothes hit the floor. Inside the shower, he let the hot water run over his face, then down his back. The heat penetrating his taut muscles, loosening their strain. He had no idea he had been holding so much tension in his body. With the crazy driving in the heavy downpours and the two guys chasing him, it seemed like days since his muscles had a chance to unwind. The little bottle of shampoo smelled of roses and imitation sandalwood. He didn't give a damn what it smelled like. His goal was to feel clean, no longer stinking like a street bum. The little square of soap on his skin washed away layers of dirt and sweat, leaving behind clean, fresh flesh. After washing away the filth, he stood under the water, letting more hot water seep into his tired flesh and bones.

Dried off and only sporting a towel wrapped around his waist, he did a thorough search of the bedding and mattress, looking for bed bugs and lice. Assured there were none, he sat down on the edge of the bed and flopped backward on the pulled-out blankets. His stomach rumbled for food, while his mind and body demanded rest. With no food available, he simply closed his eyes and let his exhausted body take him over. Feeling somewhat safe, he listened to the rain falling on the roof. He would hide Heather's notebook tomorrow. Within minutes, its soft soothing sound lulled him, making him drift off to sleep, his feet still hanging over the side of the bed.

TWO

"Is he out yet?" Gord didn't need to look up. The scent of her body arrived before her words did. She smelled of almond, on the verge of becoming sweet cherry, like fragrant Christmas marzipan. He inhaled deeply, wanting to remember her fragrance forever.

"No. You want me to bang on the door?" The motel housekeeper asked, even though she really didn't want to be the one to do it. She had done it five times in the past, each one a scary discovery. And it being room 13 didn't help matters.

Gord wasn't happy about the new guy staying pass check out time but beyond hammering on his door, there really wasn't anything he could do about it at that point. "Nah. Let him be." He looked up from his paperwork, smiling into her face, making direct contact with her dark eyes. At that moment, Maizie looked as beautiful as her first day on the job. He also felt himself yearning for her as he had back then. 'Focus,' he scolded himself. He stood up and leaned against the counter so his eyes were level with hers. "He's a traveling salesman. Looked tired as hell last night. That kinda tired that takes days to make right. Besides, I know he has money on him so I can shake him down if I need to." He saw her face light up at the mention of money. "He had a big roll of twenties in his pocket. An interesting man our new Mr. Smith."

Her face cracked a grin at the name. "Mr. Smith?"

Gord only nodded that the man in room 13 had dared to give him a fake name. "Gabriel, not John."

She laughed at his joke, then added, "Okay, I'll check on Mr. Smith again after supper." She waited for him to say something else to her — nothing came. So, she prodded him, "Have you thought about what I said?"

Gord's right eye twitched. He didn't like his staff trying to run HIS motel. Especially when it involved spending money on the rundown dump he was intending to sell the very next spring. However, he wanted to impress her. To make her like him for being more than her boss. So he lied, making it appear as though he was interested in her plans for HIS motel. "I haven't forgotten. That's why I'm looking at the books right now. And if you leave me be, I can get back to seeing if there's any extra funds for your little project."

The last two words hit a nerve. It wasn't her 'little project,' it was a plan to upgrade the motel from tired and tattered — to new and fresh — and a little closer to the current century. Remodeling that would ensure a steady stream of new customers, bringing a steady stream of profits. Instead of protesting, which would have fallen on deaf ears anyway, she kept her argument to herself. She swallowed down her frustration, "Okay, then. See you later." She turned and left the office with her cart, trying to neither scream nor cry.

He watched her push the housekeeper's cart down the sidewalk to the room in the left elbow of the motel courtyard. To him, she was beautiful. Glossy black hair and caramel skin. Not too slim with curves in all the right places. The problem was — she was half his age. A fact, she reminded him the last time he made a pass at her. She was twenty-six, he was sixty-one, and therefore over the hill in her young eyes. Too bad his libido didn't know that. It was doing just fine for an old guy.

She disappeared inside the storage room, closing the door behind her. He returned to his task at hand, doing the daily deposits and balancing the books for months end. Although it had been a reasonable tourist season during the summer months — with that spring's rainy months he hadn't made as much money as he needed to carry them on. He was hoping like hell that the upcoming hunting season would pull them through. But if the fall weather was as dreadful as the spring, he would have to sell the motel fast before his creditors came knocking. He rubbed his forehead with his fingers, massaging the tension away.

'That roll of twenties would come in handy,' he thought to himself. He wasn't suggesting he steal it from Mr. Smith. He was thinking more along the lines of Gabriel paying the same 'special' rate for the remainder of his stay. And by the numbers on the tally sheet in front of him, he needed to do his best to make him stay on as long as he could. He would even let Mr. Smith hide his car in his garage for few extra bucks.

~

Gabriel had heard the banging on his door. The knocks very faint at first, then increasingly harder when he didn't answer. He stayed laying on the bed, pulling the blankets over his naked body, more out of self-modesty than warmth. He didn't care that it was past check out time. He wasn't ready to get up, let alone leave the comfort of the soft motel mattress. He was staying right where he was, going back to sleep — forever, if he could.

What was the point of getting up? So he could worry about Rene and Cash chasing him down to shoot him in the head? He was tired of running. Tired of looking over his shoulder for the two faces in the crowd that were about to kill him. He was tired to the bone. Tired of not getting enough sleep or food to maintain his strength.

Food.

His stomach ached at the mere thought of it. Yet he was simply too exhausted to move. He rolled over, burying his face into the pillow to block out the light creeping under the heavy green curtains. She finally left, pushing the squeaky little cart down to the next door. He heard her unlock the door and begin to clean the room beside him. She hummed as she worked. 'The sign of a happy employee,' thought Gabriel. He heard sheets being removed from the bed, the headboard softly thudding on the shared wall. Next came the sound of her vacuuming.

The vacuum head hits something else hard several times, his body jumping with each startling impact.

The bangs triggered his memory, bringing him back to the night Rene was kicking in the motel room just outside Port Hope. He barely escaped that night. Just making it out the bathroom window when the door came crashing in.

Feeling his body tense up with each flashback, he became aware of how tormented his life had become. His body had trained itself to feel fear at the sound of everyday noises. His instinctive sense of 'fight-or-flight' always picking the latter. Last came the sound of water running and the toilet flushing. She was still humming when she locked the door behind her. The cart squeaked away, fading out of his hearing range.

His stomach growled again, demanding it be fed. When was the last time he had eaten? Sault Ste Marie? No, he was running for his life from there. Wawa? Yes, on his first time through. A greasy burger and a pop by the big Canadian Goose. He hid amongst the tourists waiting to take their pictures with the twenty-eight-foot bird. That was nearly three days ago. Food had become the priority of the morning. 'Day,' he reminded himself since he had slept through the entire morning.

Remembering Gord's instructions about finding phone numbers on the mirror, Gabriel made himself sit up in bed, letting his mind get its bearings within the gloom of the unfamiliar room. Turning the light on, he shuffled his feet to the desk and leaned forward to read the squares of paper taped to the mirror. Not only were there numbers, but Gord had provided a takeout menu from the local restaurant itself. Kathi's Kitchen offered a variety of takeout dishes. Everything from burgers to breakfast. But what really caught his eye was the word lasagna. Instantly he knew that's what he would order to satisfy both his stomach and his taste buds. But first, he needed to make himself presentable. He dressed his naked body with his only clean white t-shirt and the same jeans he had worn for the last 6 days. He dialed the number and cleared his throat before they answered.

"Kathi's Kitchen. What can I get ya?" The woman's voice was nasal and a somewhat frazzled.

"Afternoon ma'am. I'd like to make a takeout order."

Not recognizing his voice as one of her regulars, "Sure thing. What's your name?"

"Gabriel ... Smith," he corrected, maybe just a little too quickly.

"Okay, Gabriel Smith. What do you want?" her tone of voice revealed she was trying to be patient with him, even though she was up to her elbows in orders.

"I'll take your lasagna. One order." Why he said that, he had no idea.

"You want salad or garlic bread with that?" she offered flatly, as though she had said it a thousand times too many. "It's extra."

"Nope. Just the lasagna." He heard the kitchen bell ring in the background, meaning orders were up and ready to be delivered.

"And where to?"

"Last Motel. Room thirteen."

19

"Thirteen!" she snorted on the other end. After a few seconds, she cleared her throat, becoming professional again, "Okay. You got cash? We don't do that fancy portable debit machine."

"Yes, ma'am, I do have cash."

Her tone turned adamant, "No hundreds. We don't take them after I got ripped off last fall."

"I've got small bills." He paused for a second, "Can you add a strawberry milkshake to that order?"

"Can do." She scribbled it down. "Is that all?"

"No, that's good. How long?"

"It's our special of the day so it's pretty much ready to go. I'd say, twelve minutes, tops."

"Great. Can't wait ... I'm starving."

She chuckled, "Been a lot of that around here today. Well, 'til they leave that is." She laughed hard in the mouthpiece, making Gabriel pull his receiver away from his ear. "Okay, it'll be there in about twelve. Bye."

After hanging up, he hunted through his pants pocket for a ten, three ones, and a two. By his quick calculations, fifteen dollars was enough to cover the bill and a hefty tip too. Always good to keep delivery boys on your good side. He kind of made the bed and brushed his hair, trying to not look so pathetic to the delivery kid. He sat in the motel chair, staring at the back of the door, waiting patiently for his hot, filling food to arrive. He thought about the rich red sauce and the soft noodles. He hoped the ground beef was garlicky and there was lots of cheese on top. His stomach growled at him for teasing it with mental pictures of all the lasagnas he had eaten over the years.

When the knock came, he swore he could smell the garlicky tomato sauce through the thick motel door. His mouth watered at just the thought of it. Still in survival mode, he grabbed his backpack and tucked it under the blankets. Being extra cautious, he peeked through the curtain's crack, making sure it wasn't Rene or Cash. What he saw at the door surprised him. It was no pimple faced teenaged boy. Waiting patiently was a twenty-something tall blonde, her skin pale with a spray of rusty freckles over her cheeks and nose. Her jeans were tight and her t-shirt clung to her slim curves.

"Kathi's Kitchen," she yelled through the door, knocking hard again.

He slid the chain and opened the door only half-way, exchanging the brown paper bag with his money. In the background, he saw the housekeeper pushing her cart down the other half of the motel complex. She was also looking his way. "Keep the change as tip. Thank you," was all he said to the delivery girl, closing the door quickly, replacing the chain.

The delivery girl, Dani, counted the money in her hands. There was indeed a big tip. With the bill being just under twelve dollars, that left an extra three-dollar tip. Too bad she had to share it with everyone else at the restaurant. 'Or maybe not,' she thought, stuffing the two in her back pocket, keeping it for herself.

Inside, Gabriel ripped open the bag, praying that they had included a fork and knife. They had. A large mouthful was sucked through the oversized straw of the milkshake.

Blended ice cream had never tasted so good. Cold, sweet, and very strawberry. He felt it go down his throat and land in his empty stomach. He put that down and started to pry the lid off the pasta dish. Unfolding of the aluminum container's edge seemed to take forever.

Once he got the lid completely off, he held the shiny side of it to his mouth and licked off any trace of sauce or cheese it held. The container itself was hot on his skin but he didn't care, he wasn't waiting, he was so hungry he had to eat right then. He pulled the little chair over to the bed, sat in it and put his feet up. Forkful after forkful he shoved in, barely swallowing what was in his mouth before the next hunk went in. He moaned at the rich deep flavor of the tomato sauce. He moaned at the stretchy, gooey cheese on top. He was two-thirds done the dish, when it hit him. He had eaten too fast, his stomach balking at his haste. More rich creamy milkshake went in. Again, his stomach protested. He conceded that he would have to slow down or throw up what he had just gorged. Smaller bites being chewed longer before swallowing seemed to please his gut. At that moment, he had never tasted anything so delicious in his entire life. Taking his time, he savored every last bite and loud slurp.

Overfull and very content, he put the chair back and returned to the bed, laying back, his hands tucked behind his head. Gabriel let out a long relaxing sigh. He could feel energy slowly returning to his body. His mind was becoming clearer. His thoughts able to sort themselves out. Untangling the mess, his mind had become. All of it was what his body and brain had required. Food, rest and quiet. He lay still, enjoying the comfort of being safe and full.

As quickly as his 'energy high' came, it slipped down the other side. His eyes became heavy and his breathing shallow. With his leg against his backpack still beneath the blankets, he was asleep within twenty minutes, snoring loudly. His arms unconsciously lowered to cross his chest, forming an imaginary shield against his own fears.

~

Maizie was done for the day — except for the laundering of the sheets and towels. All the rooms but room 13 had been cleaned and made up. She did manage to get a quick peek at Mr. Smith when Dani delivered his food. He was holding the door open but not wide enough for her to see inside. She was worried he didn't have enough clean towels or shampoo. But that was Maizie, she worried about everything that happened at the motel.

She loved her job and her little motel suite. For her, it was a shrunken version of a real home. It had a small living room and an even smaller kitchen. But it was all hers. She didn't have to share it with her sisters — or an abusive drunk asshole of a boyfriend. To her happiness, Gord had said she could do whatever she wanted to her own room, including painting the walls. He had only stopped by once to see what she had done to the place.

When she gave him a tour of the room, he was surprised at how different it looked from its original sad state of beige and avocado. She watched as he marveled at the makeshift wall of curtains that surrounded her bed, separating it from the couch and throw rug area, which Maizie called the living room. The walls were painted a pale grey with white trim — a very classy style for his old run-down motel. She had even covered the couch with a fabric that coordinated with the curtain wall. A heavy fabric that was a classic black, white, and grey motif. He said he loved what she had done and that he was impressed with her designing skills. That's when she hinted that he should do that to all the rooms at the motel. She could transform one room at a time, making each room the same as hers. She even offered to get all the supplies and do all the work herself. All he had to do was come up with the money for those supplies — and wages for her extra hours of work. All he replied was that he would have to check the books to see if there was extra money for such a project. That's where it was left — no commitment, just a big fat 'MAYBE.' She had been working on her grand plan for some time. All she needed was Gord to say he had the money and she could start rejuvenating the old motel.

Her mind wandered back to the strange man in room 13. Seeing Gabriel through his doorway was a shock to Maizie. The man was hairier than any man she had ever seen. Almost shoulder length scraggly hair and a scruffy untrimmed beard. Why Gord thought he was a traveling salesman made no sense to her. No one would buy anything from someone who looked that disheveled and unprofessional. Even most of the miners and lumbermen

Maizie knew, kept themselves tidier than Mr. Smith had. She was also curious as to why he closed the door so fast. Most men took their time when talking to sexy Dani. And for Dani, it had become a sport in getting them to ask her out. 'A free meal is a free meal,' she would laugh with the girls. Meaning she'd go out with them to dinner, not caring if she liked the guy or not. But Mr. Smith didn't talk to Dani. He shoved the money at her and closed the door in her face. 'He didn't even look at her legs or ass. Maybe he don't like girls,' she supposed, then laughed at her own ridiculous thoughts.

Whatever the man's reasons were for being so secretive, they were none of her business. Her job was to clean rooms and nothing more. Except that was not true when it came to her future plans. Plans that hinged on Gord accepting her proposals and upgrading the motel. As much as she wished it would happen, she also braced herself for a big fat NO from her boss. She could accept a NO answer, understanding that business had been lousy lately. But if it was a YES — well that answer would change her life completely. She would then become the motel's interior designer. No longer just the housekeeper. She sighed at how close she was to becoming something besides a manual worker. Becoming a professional. Too bad it was all in the hands of a man that didn't like to part with his money.

She walked to the front window of her room and peeked out the white sheers. She looked out across the motel's courtyard, her mind still wondering who the man in room 13 was. Why the quick retreat into his room? But more importantly — why he was there in her shitty little town in the middle of nowhere? Her guts told her there was more to his story — a story she wasn't sure she wanted to know about.

THREE

Her workday started around eight in the morning — another great benefit of being a motel housekeeper. Her first stop was the front office to see which rooms had emptied during the night or earlier that morning. Once she had the list, she started her work for the day.

The job itself was boring beyond belief. No one ever got excited about changing dirty sheets or cleaning up toothpaste spit and God-knows-what in the bathtub. Occasionally, some kind soul would leave some cash on the bed or desk as an apology for the horrendous mess they had left behind. But those were very few in the run-down motel. Absurdly, most people seemed to 'clean' their rooms before they checked out — leaving behind some comical bed-making techniques. Why they did it, Maizie had no idea. Did they not understand that the sheets would be stripped off and replaced every day? Just because the motel was old and rundown, didn't mean it was filthy. It was her job to make sure fresh linens were placed on each bed and that each room was properly cleaned to not only her satisfaction but that of their region's health board. But no one was tougher on Maizie, than Maizie. She worked tirelessly to go further than the standards, maintaining healthy, spotless rooms for their guests.

Once inside room 5, she locked the door behind her and slipped on her Walkman headphones. Working to the beat of her favorite music made her mundane job go by faster. She always did the rooms in a specific order. One, to minimize the workload. And two, to make sure she didn't stress her body, avoiding injuries. Specifically, circumventing a back injury, a common affliction amongst housekeepers. She couldn't get injured on the job. If she did, and it was permanent, she would not only lose her job, she would lose her home as well. Maizie was determined not to live on the streets again — the cold, cruel life she had left three years ago. She did her best to stay right where she was, safe and dry with a job she somewhat enjoyed.

The work was so repetitive, she did it without really acknowledging it. Instead, her mind was busy planning for the motel's future — her future. She was thinking about the next steps to use with Gord. A presentation that would prove her suggestions would increase business and make greater profits than what he was currently bringing in. Visual proof that with a little investment by him, the motel could be upgraded — no, RENEWED — to a more modern motel.

Her latest scheme included a package for honeymooners, rather than hunters. Five days/four nights at a cut rate that also included coupons from a few of the gift shops and restaurants in town. A good way to fill all the rooms, instead of only half of them.

The last thought filled her face with a sappy grin. With the current number of 'permanent guests' there were fewer rooms available for the 'visiting guests.' Maizie was not knocking the 'permanent guests' who paid by the month. They were the motel's bread and butter. Without them, she knew the motel would be in deep financial trouble.

Yet she was sure that once she renovated the first four rooms, along with some online advertising, they would be able to attract a better class of guest. City people and honeymooners that had money to spend.

She tossed the dirty sheets into the bin on the end of the cart. A fresh flat sheet snapped out over the mattress and folded under at all four corners. The next flat sheet floated over top, slowly landing in place over a cushion of air. The foot end was tucked in place while the top edge was lined up with the top of the pillows. Next came the freshly clean bedspread. She hated them. They were old, ugly, and faded. 'Kinda like this motel,' she often thought. She promised herself that they would be the first things to go. Straight in the garbage where they should have been tossed about ten years ago. She unhooked the vacuum and plugged it in, the loud sucking sound drowning out the music in her earphones.

The problem she was contemplating was troubling. What to do with the 'permanent guests' that didn't want to move from their current room to another 'new and improved' room. She knew the old lady in room 10 would happily comply since she was always complaining about the man next door and his annoyingly loud TV. And in thinking of room 11, she knew Mr. Moses would also like to move — as far away from Tula as possible! Maizie couldn't confirm it, but she was pretty sure the two of them had shared a night of passion and one of them didn't want to take it any further. She chuckled at the thought of the two old coots going at it in bed.

Done vacuuming, she turned her attention to the cleaning of the bathroom. The room had been occupied by a millwright from Sudbury. He was there to fix a machine thing-a-ma-dooey for the mine just north-east of town. He had only stayed there for the two days and had requested that his room NOT be cleaned while he was away. That only meant one thing — he was hiding a secret behind the lock of his door. He wasn't the first to do it and he wouldn't be the last. Generally, it was a drug habit they thought they needed to worry about. Only once had Maizie refused to go into a room to clean it after she opened the door.

~

She could smell it in the air before she saw it on the bedding. The sheets had blood on them. Streaks of dried burgundy that didn't look natural. Far too much for it to be blood from menstruation. And besides, it was a man staying there, not a female. Instead of going inside, she locked the door again to preserve the scene and went straight to the office to tell Gord what she had found. At first, he didn't believe her, thinking she was being overly dramatic. But after she described the gory scene again and begged him to call the police, he took her fears seriously.

He grabbed his copy of the master key and headed to the room. Opening the door long enough to confirm what she had told him, he quickly closed it and ran back to the office to call the local OPP. He wasn't happy that the police were at his motel, setting the local rumor mill running at full throttle. Police — Blood — Motel. That was a recipe for murder even if there wasn't a body to be found. After a thorough investigation, blood samples were sent off to be tested. It was discovered that the blood was animal and not human. The police determined the person staying there was considered mentally deranged and had a history of using feral cats in some sort of animal ritual. Maizie almost vomited when Gord repeated what the cops had told him. For the local gossipers, it was a bigger story than what their small-town imaginations could contrive. Everything from scantily-clad witches to blood-thirsty werewolves practicing some sort of hedonistic ceremony in that room. Who's cat he had killed and used, no one ever knew? The room still gave Maizie the creeps.

~

With the toilet cleaned and the sink rinsed, she tackled the tub/shower combo. There in the bottom of the tub sat a white washcloth soaked in some sort of purple liquid. What that purplish liquid was she wasn't sure. Still wearing her rubber gloves, she pinched it high into the air and sniffed it from a distance. Blueberry tea. "Freaks," she cursed to herself, tossing it into a separate plastic bag for bleaching later. A good dowsing of bleach splashed in the bottom of the tub, bleeding the purplish stain down the drain when she opened the shower head. She turned her attention to the floor. It was the last job in the bathroom, leaving no prints on the wet floor as she mopped herself out of the room.

With all the dust from vacuuming settled, she took out her damp dusting cloth and wiped down every surface of the room. She noticed the picture that hung between the two beds was on a slight slant. She stepped up on the mattress and carefully lifted the picture off the wall. As she suspected, there was a new addition to the original "picture on the back." The guest had added horns to the naked lady with the extra nipple and snakes coming out of her crotch. "People are batshit crazy," she muttered as she re-hung it. Maizie got back to work with a quick wipe of the mirror screwed to the wall above the desk.

She tossed the cloth on top of the cart. The final step was to spray every surface with disinfectant. She slid her earphones off and let them rest on her neck, still listening to her music, barely a whisper. Unlocking the door, she moved on to the next room that needed cleaning. The cycle repeating itself all over again.

Pushing her cart to the seventh room, the motel's laundry room, to drop off the dirty linens. As she sorted the linens into separate piles, she wondered if the man in room 13 was going to allow her in today. She needed to clean his room — or at least replace his dirty towels for fresh ones. To her housekeeper senses, she was conflicted inside about the shaggy man she saw through the crack of the door. Was he really just a wary traveling salesman resting his exhausted body? Or was there more to his story? Either way, she wasn't looking forward to meeting him. Not after the reaction she got from Gord. He said very little about the man. A sign that he was hiding information that he felt Maizie didn't need to know. With a load of linens leftover from yesterday still in the machine done, she transferred it into the dryer. She unloaded the new pile of dirty sheets into the washer. The blueberry stained washcloth she added to a pail of luke-warm water, detergent, and bleach. A good overnight soak and it would be bright white again.

Next stop was Tula's room — always a surprise waiting there. What it would be on this weekly visit, Maizie only wondered. She didn't get a chance to knock on the door, Tula yanked it open before her knuckles hit the metal.

"Come on in dear. You're early today." Tula held the door while Maizie lifted the cart over the threshold with a grunt.

"Not that many guests right now so a light workload." She looked around, her eyes looking for signs of personal neglect. But it appeared as it always was. All flat surfaces were covered with old takeout containers, empty whiskey bottles, and paper coffee cups. Tula was in her late 70's and had no desire to cook for herself any longer. All her meals were ordered in, and that meant a lot of takeout containers. For Maizie, that was her first job in Tula's room — disposing of the garbage before she could do her real job. They talked as she slid the white cardboard, empty booze bottles, and foam containers into two separate garbage bags. One for recycling, a new venture for the small town. The second bag for true garbage, such as dark-colored coffee cups and old crusty food of half-eaten meals. The last container of food reeked of moldy sweet and sour chicken, making Maizie's body shutter. Once the bags were knotted and stowed away on her cart, she started to strip down the bed. She ignored the yellow stain in the middle of the sheet, knowing a good bleaching would take that out, leaving it fresh white again. This was a regular routine with Tula and her elderly bladder. Maybe she should clean her room twice a week, instead of only the once.

"So, who's the new guy in the cat room? I saw you knocking on his door but he didn't come out." She batted her eyes flirtatiously, "Is he an older gentleman, by chance?"

Maizie chuckled at Tula's ability to narrow in on what information she wanted and why. She sprayed the plastic mattress cover with disinfectant, choking on the fine moist droplets that remained suspended in the air. "I haven't seen him yet myself." Off came the pillowcases. "But Gord says his in his early thirties." She snapped out the bottom flat sheet, laying it flat across the bed. "So, unless he's into older women, you're out of luck."

"Dang it!" She crossed her legs and swung her foot angrily, "How's a girl supposed to get some before she croaks."

This statement didn't shock Maizie, she'd heard the senior say a lot worse in her company. "You just hang in there then. Your white knight is coming any day now."

"Oh, make fun if you want but when you get this age, the days have more meaning." Her foot stopped, "You want to get a few last things in before the grim reaper comes a calling."

With all four corners tucked in and tightly secured, on went the top flat. She knew Tula liked her sheets tucked in all the way up the left side but only halfway up the right side. The things she did for these people made her both laugh and groan. As much as it pleased her heart to make them feel at home in the crappy motel, it also irked her that they often took advantage of her and Gord's generosity. Maizie sniffed the bedspread. "You okay with this? Or should I wash it?"

"Nah, it's good. Didn't use it this past week so no mishaps on it."

"You're sure? It's no trouble to chuck it in the wash with the others."

"That's my worry ... the others. God knows what's on them."

'Good point,' thought Maizie. She didn't say it though. She didn't want to go down that path of scolding and bitching about Gord letting in all manner of depraved humans stay at his motel — referring to 'the Cat incident' in room 13 as a point of reference. She folded it in half, the ugly avocado print put together. A quick snap made it lay flat on top of the sheets, a simple unfolding of the other half into its proper place. A trick she learned from a well-seasoned motel maid as a way to avoid putting excess stress on her back. "How's the bathroom? You need a good clean in there?" The answer from the elderly women was always NO. Maizie knew better though. She inspected the room from the doorway, "Nope, I'm sorry. I can't leave it like this for another week. It'll only take me a few minutes to get it up to my standards." She didn't wait for an answer, she just went to work, cleaning everything and replenishing the towels. She checked the toilet paper supply under the sink. As it had been for the last four weeks, Tula had not used any of the rolls of toilet paper. Maizie's body shivered at the thought of what she was using to wipe her behind. The bigger part of her did not want to know. But the responsible, caring part of her heartfelt she needed to find out before it became a health issue for the motel itself. She was about to ask the senior when it started again.

The sound of the TV next door, blasting through the walls. Moses was watching his afternoon sports recap — at full volume. She came out of the bathroom just in time to see Tula jump from her chair and hammer her frail fists on the shared wall.

"TURN THAT DOWN YOU OLD GOAT!" She waited for the volume to go down and when it didn't, she yelled again. "I SAID ... TURN IT DOWN!!" Again, she listened, this time her ear pressed against the wall. As before, the TV continued to blare through the thin walls. She turned on Maizie, yelling at her instead, "MAKE THAT OLD COOT TURN IT OFF."

"You know I can't ask him to turn it off. But I can ask him to turn it down though. Just sit down and I'll be right back." Maizie exhaled an exasperated sigh, "You two got to stop this fighting."

"Well, he starts it." Her finger pointed towards the dividing wall. "With that damned TV OF HIS!"

Maizie left her yelling at the wall. She knocked hard on room 11, hoping Moses would hear it over the loud TV. When he didn't come to the door, she did what Tula did, she yelled through it. "MOSES! IT'S ME, MAIZIE! OPEN THE DOOR!" She heard the volume go down, meaning he was trying to hear what she had said. "Moses, It's me Maizie. Open the door."

The lock tripped and he let it open wide. "What do YOU want?" His voice was snarly, defensive — and extremely loud. "You come to give me hell again?"

She changed her expression to one of compassion, "Now Moses, don't be like that." She had to half yell for him to hear, "As they say, 'Don't kill the messenger.' Besides, it is my job to keep peace."

"Is that old bitty still trying to tell me what to do? Nosy old bitch."

"I HEARD THAT!" came from the room next door.

Maizie just closed her eyes at the whole situation, inhaling deeply to keep herself calm before she went forward as moderator. This fight had gone on long enough, there had to be a solution.

Tula griped, "Why can't you put him in another room?"

"WHY CAN'T YOU PUT THE WITCH IN ANOTHER ROOM?" he countered at full volume, stabbing his finger towards the voice on the other side of the wall.

"I WAS HERE FIRST ... YOU GOD DAMN MOVE!"

It was the exact same fight they had every damned time. They were acting like spoiled bickering children and Maizie was sick of it. "Come with me," she ordered Moses. He followed her outside to the front sidewalk. "Tula, get out here. NOW!" she bellowed over the TV. When the two of them were standing before her, she laid out the new rules for them. "I have had it. As of now, this feud of yours has reached its end." They both inhaled to state their case to the housekeeper but she didn't let them begin their list of complaints. "Don't want to hear it." Her halting finger stopped the next attempts. She faced the old man, "From now on, Moses, you will keep the volume down." She turned to Tula, "And you will be patient with his hearing loss." They both inhaled to complain again and she stopped them cold with the next sentence, "Because whoever complains to me again, will be moved into room 13." The look of shock filled both their faces. "I mean it. I am tired of being your referee. Behave or I'll move you to the cat room."

A finger pointed, "But she ..."

"Are you complaining Moses?" She looked him right in the eyes, "Are you?"

"You can't do that," protested Tula.

"Watch me," she said bluntly.

His arms crossed his chest, "Gord will never let you do that."

"Gord told me to." It was a bold-faced lie but she could square it away with Gord, covering her ass.

Tula didn't say much more. She returned to her room and sat in her chair, slumped over, as though scolded and defeated.

A gruff 'harrumph' was all she got from Moses before he returned to his room.

Maizie let out a heavy sigh, praying her threat would put an end to their bickering. But knowing those two, she doubted it. Although it was never said, she knew damned well it was more than his loud TV that riled Tula. She was ninety percent sure they were once lovers that broke up in a not so friendly manner. Whatever the problem was, she wanted the hostility to stop.

She put on a big smile and with her cheeriest voice, asked Tula to cooperate, "I have to vacuum now. Up on the bed with you." That was their routine since the day Maizie accidentally hit Tula's baby toe with the vacuum cleaner, turning it into a big blue bulb.

Vacuuming done, she gave everything a thorough wiping down, leaving behind dust free shiny surfaces. She loaded the last item on her cart and sent Tula a happy smile, "I'll see you next week. If you need something in the meantime, you know where to find me." When she closed the door behind her cart, she was sure the old woman was sticking her tongue out at her.

The next room to clean belonged to Moses. She prepared herself for more attitude from the senior. The door was still open. Moses was sitting on the edge of his chair, watching the TV, his eye squinting to hear better.

Maizie knocked on the door out of politeness, "Hey Moses, you ready for me?"

His arms still across his chest, he just glanced her way, his expression angry and shut down.

"Oooo-kay." As she began to strip down the bed, she looked around the room, wondering if there was anything she could do to change the situation between the two rooms. There was. Moving the TV away from the shared wall and onto the opposite side would be best. But it would be a lot of work moving everything around to accommodate that simple switch. Maybe if she could find someone else to help her, she'd consider it. There was no way she was going to do it by herself, possibly injuring her back. Her mind wandered over to the man in room 13. He could help her. If he stayed around long enough, that is. She took her time changing the sheets and bedspread before vacuuming. She ignored the dirty look she got from Moses when the sound drowned out his football play by play. With the dusty jobs out of the way, she braced herself for Moses's bathroom.

Of all the bathrooms she had cleaned in the motel, Moses's bathroom was the worst. The man had no concept of flushing regularly. Nor did he seem to aim at the bowl when he urinated. And that week he had not bothered to keep the towels off the floor, leaving a mildew smell in the bathroom — and in the damp towels themselves. 'More bleach,' she cursed in her head. She stuffed those in a plastic bag so they wouldn't contaminate the other linens. After twenty minutes of scrubbing, washing, and rinsing off, the bathroom was its sparkling self again. Back in the room, she set herself to dusting — and the making of amends with Moses.

She stopped what she was doing and watched the TV, her hands holding the rag in front of her bellybutton, "Who's winning?"

He gave her a sideways scowl, "No one. It's highlights from the weekend."

"Oh." She altered her question, "So who won this weekend then."

He straightened up in his chair. "I know you're just trying to be nice to me now. Just so I don't go ask Gord about what you threatened." His eyes watched her closely, looking for any sign that she was telling a lie.

She kept her face cheerful, "Threatened is such an ugly word. How about we use 'warned' instead." Then she set her eyes on his, boring into them. "Well if you're going to complain to Gord, you might as well bring Tula with you. That way Gord can raise both your rents at the same time."

His mouth dropped open. He wasn't expecting that as the answer she would give.

"Been over a year since he raised your rents last. Dew anytime now. Especially if someone reminds him." She let her statement linger in the air, pressing down on him. She tossed her dusting cloth on top of the cart and bid him goodbye. "I'm all done, Moses. As always if you need something, don't hesitate to ask."

She left out the door, the way she came, closing the door behind her. Again, she was sure the old man was giving her some type of lude gesture behind that door.

THE LAST MOTEL

Possibly both his middle fingers. Honestly, she didn't care. If her renovation plans worked out, the two of them would be at opposite ends of the motel. Neither one able to bother the other.

The next room to clean was room 13.

Lucky 13 — that is, unless you're a cat.

FOUR

She stopped her cart beside door 13 but waited for a few moments to gather her nerves. She was caught between wanting to clean the room and seeing the odd man face to face. She wasn't sure she was ready for the latter. As the day before, knocking softly at first then increasing how hard she knocked the next time. Her soft plea came through the door, "Mr. Smith. Are you awake? I need to clean your room." She waited for his answer.

His voice was deeper than she assumed it would be. "Yes, I'm in. And NO, I don't want my room cleaned."

"At least let me change your sheets. Please, let me in." When he didn't respond again, she gave up and knocked softly once more, "Sir, I'm going to leave some towels and bathroom toiletries outside your door. In case you need fresh towels and stuff." She laid them down on the plastic chair and returned to her cleaning cart. with her tone cheery yet slightly phony, she ended their encounter, "Enjoy your stay at The Last Motel."

Lord how she hated to say that name out loud. Yet for her it was a job that not only paid her well, it also provided her with a permanent place to live. A clean warm home that was far-away from her previous life of living on the streets in Sault Ste Marie. A life in the Soo she tried very hard not to return to.

It was Gord who found her, sleeping under a park bench. She had curled up underneath it for protection against thieves and rapist. He was kind, thoughtfully offering her a hot cup of coffee along with a Styrofoam container of fish and chips. A duplicate of his own meal. He sat with her as they both ate, sharing the white cup of dark brown chemical gravy. At first, they talked about the unseasonal weather and the changes they made to the local shopping mall. Casual chit-chat until Gord got around to asking the questions he really wanted answers to. Where was she originally from? Why was she on the streets? Had she worked somewhere before? And the deal breaker — did she have a criminal record?

With each inquiry, she pondered her answer cautiously, being careful that she didn't give him too much information from her past. She answered his questions in a manner that offered facts, but not many details. He didn't need to know the reason she left her apartment was because her boyfriend would drink to excess and beat her just to ease the heaviness of his constant angry ego. To tell the stranger of her past life would be to tell him she was weak, vulnerable to anyone stronger than herself. She didn't tell him that she had been taken to jail three times for stealing. Each offense thrown out of court for lack of evidence since Maizie had eaten the food in the stores before leaving. Hunger makes a person do things they normally wouldn't. Actions that people must do to simply survive another day on the streets. Had she worked before? Yes, many places she boasted between forks of French fries and battered fish. She worked at a famous Canadian coffee chain, giving her experience with face to face customer service. A ticket taker at a movie theater, so she was great at making change. And her favorite job — a cleaning lady for ten clients after leaving high school. Not just cleaning to look clean — doing a thorough job was important to her.

Her words were like choir music to Gord. He offered her a job on the spot. For her to come to his motel, The Last Motel, to be his housekeeper. He offered minimum wage at first, along with a room of her own — rent free. No strings attached. If she worked out after a month, he would give her a dollar raise and see what he could do about getting her a car to use. Not to keep, but to use for both herself and picking up supplies from either in town or from the city. That's why he was there in the Soo, he explained. To pick up a load of toilet paper, more business cards and a new bar fridge that broke down in one of the kitchenette rooms. Gord saw the apprehensive look on her face when he offered to drive her back to the motel that same day, setting her up in the job and her room. Instead, he offered an alternative mode of transportation. He gave her enough money to go, by bus, to his motel and back. He also said, if she decided against coming to see his motel, she could keep it and use the money for anything she wanted. She remembered staring at the pile of bills he was handing her. Wary of why he was being so kind to her, she hesitated at taking the money from the complete stranger. In the past, others had been kind to her, only their agendas were to lure her into their clutches, as an unsuspecting drug runner. Or worse, for sex with creepy johns — making them big profits off her body. She had been able to avoid that part of the street world. Not getting herself involved with drugs and avoiding the pimps. She'd rather starve to death then turn tricks in the front seat of cars. She had her self-respect and it was still fully intact.

When Gord got up to leave, he shook her hand in a professional manner, assuring her that he was only interested in hiring her as his housekeeper for the motel — and nothing more. He gave her one of his new business cards and joked, "It's really 103 miles to the next motel ... but 99 rolls off the tongue better." He thanked her for her company and politely said goodbye with another classy handshake. When he walked away, she nearly yelled for him to come back, that she had decided to go work for him. But she stopped herself, fearing he would want the money back. Maizie sat on the bench, her stomach full for the first time in days. A chilling breeze blew over her, telling her that winter was coming soon. A winter filled with relentless cold snowy days and nights. Always having to shuffle from one shelter to another until she could find one that wasn't full. She quickly stuffed the money inside the cup of her bra for safe keeping. When Gord climbed in his pickup truck, its side read 'The Last Motel for 99 Miles.' He was telling the truth. Immediately, Maizie began planning her walking route to the bus station to get her ticket — maybe clean herself up in the station's bathroom before boarding the bus itself. Then she wondered if there would be enough money left over to buy some 'new' clean clothes from the Sally Ann. Maizie could sense a change in her life, a shift to a new beginning. A golden metamorphosis she was ready to grab onto.

~

He sighed in relief that the housekeeper had finally left. Gabriel was in no condition to deal with anyone.

He was simply too depressed, his will to go on was even lower than the night he arrived at the motel.

He rolled over and covered his eyes with his arm, blocking out any light that crept underneath the ugly green curtains. He needed to sleep longer. Truthfully, it was all he wanted to do. To sleep until his body stopped aching. Until his head cleared of all the craziness tumbling in an endless emotionally fueled cycle. Regurgitating the same dark thoughts over and over.

If he kept sleeping, he could escape all the horrible images imprinted on his brain. He knew he couldn't stop the ache in his heart for the loss of Heather. Nothing could ever ease that devastating pain. He wanted his mind to stop torturing him with the frozen images of her being murdered before his eyes. Images that cut at him, leaving him raw with heartbreak. Tears filled his eyes as the pain of her death once again crushed down on his chest. After crying inwardly so no one would hear, he wiped away the tears from his cheeks. As it had many times before, rage overrode his sorrow, his hands turning to clenched fists placed over his eyes, blocking out the world. Heavy sobs jerked his body with each shuttering breath he exhaled. He wanted them to stop. He hammered his forehead with his closed fists, trying to make the images go away. No matter how hard he hit himself, he could not feel it over the pain in his heart. In the last three days, he had let himself cry freely, emptying the deep sorrow he had not been allowed to release before then. He had always been on the run from Rene and Cash, never giving him a moment to truly grieve his girlfriend's death. He couldn't take it any longer — wanting to end the wretched life that was left him by the killers.

~

The front wheels of the cart she left sitting on the little step of the front door. She did it on purpose, giving Gord a reason to help her. It seemed to make him happy so she indulged his need to be her hero. "Hey, Gord."

"Hey, yourself Sunshine." His usual bright smile plastered across his face. A smile reserved for only her.

"You ready for me to clean?"

He pulled up the section of counter that opened and rushed to help her. "Let me get that for you." She stepped aside, allowing him to lift it over the lip of the threshold and pull the cart through the doorway. "There you go." A pleased grin filled his face. He had come to her rescue again. Inside, he was hoping that one of these days she would give him a hug for his efforts.

"Thanks, Gord," was all she returned. She wheeled the cart through the opening and parked it by his apartment door.

Gord watched her ass move inside her tight jeans, making his heart race faster than before. 'Jesus,' he groaned in his head. He put his hands in his pocket to stop them from grabbing her fine behind. He quickly raised his eyes from her ass to her face and pretended he hadn't been doing anything wrong. "No problem."

Her cheeks started to flush with the confession she was about to tell, "Um, just so you know, I had a little run-in with Tula and Moses. Started with that same damned TV problem and kinda ended up with me telling them that whichever one complained again, gets moved to room 13."

Gord laughed, "That'll slow them down."

"Oh, there's more."

"More?"

The pink in her face turned a darker red. "Yah, I told them that if they came to you to complain about me being a bitch, that you'd raise their rent again."

"Again? Oh please. I haven't increased their monthly rate in three damned years."

"I know that. But at that moment, it was the fastest way of shutting them up." She put on a deep frown and forced torment in her big brown eyes, "Now I feel bad that I did that to them." She knew he was putty in her hands when she pouted that way — and she used it to her advantage often.

"Don't you worry about it. I know you like them and you didn't mean any harm. I'll drop by and see them in a few days. Smooth things over for you." Honestly, he'd move the moon if it made her like him more.

She smiled wide, "Oh, thank you, Gord!" She bounced in place since he seemed to enjoy that too. Lately, she was pulling out all the stops to impress the man. Making him happy so he would go along with her plans to renovate the motel. She would do anything to get her plans put in motion. Well, almost anything. She drew the line at actually having to be intimate with the man. Just the mere thought of hugging Gord made her stomach queasy.

"Can you start in the office first. I haven't tidied my room yet." Watching Maizie's round tits bounce up and down had turned him on, his groin reacting quickly.

"Gord, tidying your room is my job. Not yours." When she saw red heating his cheeks, she understood. "But this office does need cleaning for sure." She let him off the hook by pretending the office was dirty when it truly wasn't, "Look at all this dust." She swiped her finger along his desk to show him how bad it was. "I'll start in here."

All he wanted to do was kiss that fingertip — and then those soft lips of hers. He swallowed down his desire. "Yah, start in here first." He dashed by her, being careful not to bump into her. He softly closed the door behind him — and locked it.

Ignoring his weirdness, Maizie got to work. Emptying the garbage can before vacuuming so she didn't knock it over and make a bigger mess she had to clean up. With the vacuum back on the cart, she dusted every surface, lingering on the desk. Her eyes searched for her black folder. The one that contained her brief outline of what she wanted to do to the motel. It was there, under a stack of fishing magazines, dust running down the one exposed side. Her heart dropped. It seemed he wasn't interested in its contents. Had he even looked at it? Was he stringing her along, lying to her face? 'Bastard better not be,' she snarled in her head. A loud grunt came from behind Gord's door, pulling her out of her thoughts. She hastily put down the pile and returned to dusting. The last job in the office was always the same, a thorough polishing of the front counter — generally with Gord watching her ass wiggle from his desk.

Gord came out of his apartment, a sheepish look on his face. "Okay, you can go in now." He sat down in his chair, to get out of her way, his hands folded in his lap.

Maizie pushed the cart into his place, parking it at the entrance. More to keep him out, than for easy access. The first thing she noticed was the foul air. The smell of sex hung in the air. She looked over the cart at Gord. Had he just done what she thought he had done? Had the man masturbated in his room just then? Her stomach churned and she shivered at the pornographic image in her head. Immediately, she went to the window and opened it up. "Some fresh air will do this place good." She then pulled the cart forward and closed the door, leaving a small gap in it. She leaned against his dresser, bracing herself from the despicable act he may have done in her presence. It was times like those she wondered if her job was worth all the weirdness Gord inflicted on her. But she knew the answer. She had nowhere else to go, so there she would stay. At least until it became unbearable or unsafe. With a defeated heart, she continued her work. It was always the same answer — she was stuck in her own life.

On her way to the laundry room, Maizie noticed the towels had not been taken inside by the stranger in room 13. In an odd way, it made her unhappy to know he didn't have clean towels. But she knew damn well there was a bigger problem than fresh linens locked away in room 13. The man hadn't come out of his room in nearly three days. That was never a good sign. She wondered about his mental health. Depression was an overwhelming monster that could take over a person's life, its darkness never letting go its grip. She wondered if she needed to knock on his door again. To coax him out into the fresh air. She chastised herself with a frowned forehead 'You care too much about others. Stay out of it. He'll come out when he comes out.'

Behind her, she heard a truck pull in the parking lot. A new guest was arriving for the weekend. That made her heart happy. A new person to get to know. Who knows, he might be handsome and here to sweep her off her feet. "Yah and that blue Ford is his mighty stallion," she mocked herself. She shook her head as she unlocked the laundry room door, "Get real, Alootook. This is your life now." She never used her Inuit name around others, hiding her true heritage. In her world, the Inuit people were treated as second-class people. Especially, the women. They were looked down upon. Treated like disposable trash.

Luckily, her complexion was lighter than her parents. Her face not so round and flat. Even her eyes were more Whiteman than Eskimo. Not narrow slits but full round

52

eyes. Sometimes she wondered if her mother had been unfaithful to her father. Bedding a white man that resulted in her Caucasian features.

Her time on the streets had taught her one important lesson. Even though she didn't look Inuit, she acted and sounded Inuit — and that brought on troubles she didn't need. Men hassled her for sex, offering coin change for oral sex. Other people beating her up for her heritage. As far as they were concerned, she was Inuit and that was the only reason they needed to abuse her. It took her months to train herself to not be Inuit. She changed her vocal patterns. Eliminated words and phrases only the Inuit people use. She even thought she had her boyfriend fooled, until he hit her, calling her 'nothing but a dirty Eskimo slut.' She endured his abuse for almost a year before she left for the streets again. It was safer out there amongst the drug addicts and the beggars than living with his alcoholic fists. She angrily stuffed the dirty sheets in the washing machine, as though she was pushing down the pain of those events. If only she could cleanse those memories as easily as she could the sheets.

FIVE

Morning came and went with its usual routine. It was the same as the day before for Gord. He woke up alone in his apartment that was connected to the office. He dressed and started the coffee pot for the guests and himself. When the baked goods came from Kathi's Kitchen, he helped himself to a few muffins or a bagel. Paperwork and more paperwork, filled his morning.

Tula was the first to arrive for her daily extra-large cup of coffee and a bran muffin. Where she found the 24oz coffee mug in their tiny town, he'd like to know. It had become a running joke between them. Her getting her ONE cup of complimentary coffee in her oversized mug. But Tula never lingered, like the others. She headed right back to her room and her knitting. And if he knew Tula, she would add a dram of whiskey in that coffee to get her going for the day.

Moses on the other hand, clung to Gord's every word. Words that needed to be half-yelled in his direction. That morning Moses had questions he wanted answers to. "Whose car is that parked out front of the office?"

"The fella in 13." Gord added no other details since that would create more question from the nosy senior.

"How long has it been there?" He blew on his hot coffee while he waited for the answer. His old lips blew out bits of spittle with each puff of air.

"Since he arrived." The answer was sarcastic, telling the old man it was none of his business.

"Is it going to stay there? Can I park there too?"

The last thing Gord wanted was Moses's two-toned clunker parked where everyone could see it. The ugly old rust bucket visually turning away potential guests. He told Moses straight out with a stern tone, "No. I insist that you continue to park your car in front of your room like the other tenants do."

Moses didn't like that answer and protested with a half-closed right eye. "Doesn't seem fair that one customer can do it and the others can't." He casually grabbed another muffin and stuffed it in his pocket. In the old man's opinion, for the amount of rent he paid, one free muffin a day didn't seem enough.

As usual, Gord ignored his daily thievery and held up a halting hand, "Look, I promise the car will be moved by tonight. Now don't bother me about it again." He stood up from his desk and walked into his apartment, closing the door behind him as a barrier to stop the old man's questions.

Moses knowing an opportunity when he saw one, gulped down his coffee and refilled it. A cinnamon swirl bagel went in his other pocket, along with a blueberry muffin. He patted the top of that lumpy pocket, "That takes care of today's meals." He heard the knob on the door turn, telling him he needed to go. He was half-way out the door when he heard Gord's words 'are you still here?' bellowed in his direction.

From the rear office window, Gord watched the elderly man make his way across the center courtyard. 'He's getting slower,' Gord thought. Soon he would need to move to a senior's home. And knowing Tula, she'd follow him there out of spite. With them gone, that meant less permanent monthly income for the motel. More things to worry about. The sale of the motel next spring was looking more like a reality, than just a maybe. Gord's headache was returning, starting at the temples and no amount of finger massaging seemed to ease it.

He had waited all day for the man in room 13 to come out so he could get him to move his car to his room designated parking spot. Mr. Smith never showed. The situation with the strange man was dragging on too long for his liking. He unhooked the master key from the wall and slipped on his jacket. Outside he tugged his collar high against his face as protection against the fall's chilling winds. He knocked on room 13 and waited for a response. When none came, he pounded with the heel of his fist. "Mr. Smith? Are you awake? We need to talk." He waited, his ear next to the door, bent over listening for sounds from within. His big fear was that he had absconded during the night, leaving

Gord with an unpaid bill. The lock turned, making Gord pull himself upright so he didn't appear to be spying.

The door opened, but only just a sliver. Just wide enough to speak through. "Talk about what?" Gabriel mumbled, his eyes blinking rapidly against the bright light of day.

"Well, for starters, you haven't paid me for your last two days stay. And then there's the issue of your car being parked out front of my office. It needs to be moved out front of your room." He saw Gabriel's hand go upward, holding his forehead with his hand.

His voice was soft and muffled, as though he had just woken up. The door opened further, allowing Gord to see all of Gabriel's face. His eyes looked down, avoiding the motel manager, "I'll come down and pay you in a bit." He was about to close the door but Gord stuck his foot in the way.

"Now would be better." His tone told Gabriel he wasn't just suggesting it, he was ordering him to come right then.

His head nodded warily, "Yes. Yes of course." He looked Gord in the face as a sign he was giving his word. "Just let me get cleaned up and I'll be right down."

"And move the car?"

"Right after I pay you."

"Not a problem. I'll be waiting." He pulled his foot back, letting Gabriel close the door.

Gord stood where he was, hoping like hell the man on the other side wasn't lying and would show up with the money. Finally hearing the sound of running water, he left for the office. He would give him thirty minutes. After that, he would come back with the police and get him out.

Gord was still watching the clock when he saw Gabriel make his way to the office. He looked cleaner than earlier but he still needed a shave — and about six days more sleep. The man's eyes were still rimmed by dark circles and his complexion was paler than the paperwork Gord was holding in his hand. Gord had an uneasy feeling in his gut when it came to Mr. Smith. Something was definitely not normal about the man or the situation by which he came to the motel. If he wanted to stay in his motel, he'd have to tell Gord what that situation was or leave.

Gabriel opened and closed the front door quickly, attempting to hold back the brisk fall winds. He realized he would have to buy some warmer clothes in town. What little clothes he did own were of summer weight, not heavy enough for fall weather in Northern Ontario. He spoke before he got to the counter, "Afternoon."

Gord didn't feel the need to be polite to the man who hadn't paid him two nickels in two damned days. "You mean, evening."

Hearing the testiness of his voice, he decided to play nice with the man. "Guess you're right there." He wiped his hand over his mouth to add to the lie. "Sorry about not coming sooner. Been super tired. Slept most of the time."

Gord could attest to his statement since he hadn't seen much of Gabriel. And there had only been that one order of food from Kathi's Kitchen in all that time. Maybe he was telling the truth. It would also explain the fatigued state his body was in. He looked down his nose at him, "You're feeling better then?"

"A bit. Still could use some more sleep."

"And some food ..." Gord added casually.

"Yah, that too." He put his elbows on the counter and leaned forward to appear friendly, "So ... how much do I owe you?"

"Well, that depends. How much longer you wanting to stay?" He stood up and sat against the side of his desk, his arms crossed over his ribcage. "If you're staying longer, I'll need you to pay for those days up front too."

"I can appreciate that." Having made plans, Gabriel did a quick calculation in his head. "Another two days should do it."

"So, that's four days at seventy dollars a day. That equals two-hundred and eighty dollars." He dropped his arms and pointed out the front window, "And you need to move your car to your designated spot. Had a complaint about it this morning."

"A complaint?" Gabriel found it odd that someone would complain about his car being parked where it was.

"Don't worry about it. I handled it." Gord's expression made it seem like he was doing Gabriel a giant favor. "But it will have to be moved."

"Can do." Gabriel pulled out his wad of cash and started to count it out.

The sight of all the bills being counted, made his greedy side kick in. Gord cleared his throat, "Unless you want it completely out of sight?" When Gabriel nodded, he offered him his rates, "For five-dollars a day, I would park it out of sight behind the motel. For ten, I can hide it inside my garage."

Gabriel's eyes ever so slightly narrowed at his suggestion. How did Gord know he was on the run? He didn't answer him. Instead, he pushed the stack of two-hundred and eighty dollars towards him and made another pile of two five-dollar bills. "Out back is good enough."

"Then I'll need the keys." Gord scooped up the stack of cash and stuffed it in his pocket with a grin, "Unless you want to move it yourself?"

He placed the keys on the counter, "Nah. I trust you." Yet, in his head, he wondered if he really should trust a man so money hungry. But what did it matter? Once he went through with his plan, Gord could do whatever he wanted with the car. "We done here?" Gord nodded they were. "Good. 'Cause I need something to eat. Which way is Kathi's Kitchen?"

Gord pointed eastward, "Down four blocks ... on the corner." He opened the section in the counter, "You want me to drive you down?"

"Nope. I could use the fresh air."

"You tell them I sent you." He opened the door for Gabriel, "And they make some damned good soup over there. Kathi can do things with chicken and noodles even my Ma couldn't have done."

As if on cue, Gabriel's stomach growled. "Sounds good to me." As he walked, he watched Gord start the car and drive it around behind the motel. Then he aimed his weary body down the sidewalk, looking for food his starving body desperately needed.

Along the way he checked out the stores on either side of the street, taking note of the ones he would use if he was to stay around. But he wasn't sticking around — he had already decided that. Hardware store, barber shop, and a grocery store. He stopped into the little department store. Stedmans, Canada's everything store. There he bought himself a red plaid lumberjack coat. Thick wool and satin lining that would keep out the cold temperatures. He added a couple of black t-shirts, a pair of dark jeans. New underwear was also added to the pile. He paid cash and politely asked to use the change room again. Dressed in his new clothes, he felt his spirits uplift, making him feel human again. He bid his goodbyes to the friendly clerk and continued his hunt for food.

Reaching the restaurant, he looked for an open table. There were none. Every booth and table was packed with people. The sounds of coffee cups being stirred, forks on plates and the murmur of people talking filled the air. If a busy restaurant was the sign of a good restaurant, he was standing in a four-star mom and pop diner.

When the plump forty-something waitress showed up, her nasal voice told him she was the one who took his order over the phone. "Don't you worry, Hun. I'll find you a place to sit." She stood on her tip-toes, looking for available seats. "Got one. Follow me," she ordered with a small wave.

Everyone in the place checked him out as they walked by, eyeing him from baseball cap to tennis shoe. To his surprise, the tables were filled with mostly men. Men that glanced at him and whispered their opinion to each other. Words such as 'new guy,' 'motel,' and 'scruffy' found their way to Gabriel's ears.

She spoke over her shoulder, loud enough for everyone in the place to hear. "Don't mind them. They stare at all the new people in town. Nothing but a bunch of nosey parkers. Gossip more than their wives." She aimed the last sentence at a table full of elderly men. That brought a laugh from them, as they knew it was the truth.

She stopped at a table that seated one person in it. The dark-haired housekeeper from the motel. "Maizie, do you mind if this gentleman sits with you? We're plumb out of seats." Maizie nodded it was fine with her. "Well, there you go. All set then." She placed the plastic covered menu on his half of the table, "You get yourself comfortable and I'll be back to take your order."

He stopped her before she got two steps in, "Can I have a strawberry milkshake?" From her unflattering brown uniform, she took out her order pad and pen. "Please," he added out of courtesy, remembering his own student days of restaurant work.

She smiled at his politeness, "Sure thing, Hun. Be right back with that."

Gabriel took a deep breath before he sat down in the brown leatherette booth. Being out in public after so many days alone, was one thing, but sitting across from a very attractive woman he didn't know was rather nerve-racking. He put his Stedmans bag on the inside and out of courtesy to his female company, he took off his baseball cap, laying it on top of the bag. He glanced her way, trying his hardest to keep calm. "Thank you for letting me sit with you."

She glanced over his shoulder at the waitress and rolled her eyes. He watched her full lips purse her dislike at being put in that position in the first place. "Like I had a choice."

He chuckled at her, "Yah, same here." He busied himself by opening up his menu, searching for the perfect meal to fill his empty stomach. 'Talk to her,' he chastised himself. He left the menu in place as a barrier between them. He needed more time to settle his anxieties at being thrust into such an 'in your face' situation. "So, what's good on here?"

She paused in thought for a moment, then gave him her honest answer, "Everything."

He smiled wide, "That doesn't help me narrow it down." He looked over the top of his menu, examining her plate. He surmised it was the remains of a hot roast beef sandwich. He pointed at it, "Any good?"

"Not as good as mine ... but it's a damned good runner-up." She pointed to the 'Specials' board, "Mostly I got it 'cause it was cheap."

He read the other meals listed on the whiteboard and decided the number two would hit the spot. He placed the menu on the edge of the table, telling the waitress he was ready to order.

Maizie recognized the meaning of the placement as well and forewarned him, "She could be awhile." She pointed with her nose, "Place is packed and they're down one waitress." She poked at the food left on her plate with her fork, "This is normally Maggie's day off ... and she ain't too happy to be here. She was cursing earlier about missing out on her monthly shopping trip to Timmins with the girls."

Gabriel couldn't imagine what Maggie was like when she was happy, since she was currently more than pleasant to him. Or was it that he had become jaded by Toronto's serving-people with their 'what-ev-er' attitudes.

Maggie came down the aisle, milkshake in one hand, coffee pot in the other. She topped off mugs on her way. Finally reaching Gabriel, she placed his shake in front of him and the coffee pot beside it. With order pad flat on her hand and pen poised, she asked him bluntly, "What'd you want?" All the niceness had left her voice.

Aw, there was the 'unhappy' Maggie Maizie was talking about. He plastered on his friendliest smile. "I'll have the number two ... hot turkey with gravy on the mash. No cranberries."

The last part made everyone in hearing range laugh out loud. One man turned around to see who the idiot was.

"Christ on a cracker!" scoffed Maggie. "Son, we don't serve cranberries unless it's a holiday." Then she teased him, poked him in the shoulder with the inkless end of her pen, "Tell you what ... you come back at Thanksgiving and I'll give you doubles." She turned her attention to Maizie,

"You done?" Again, the two words curt, tinged with bitterness at being at work and not in Timmins.

She shifted in her seat, "No. I'm good." She knew damned well that the minute Mr. Smith's plate arrived, it would trigger her appetite again. Without another word, Maggie was off again, filling mugs on her way back to the kitchen.

They both sat awkwardly in silence, both waiting for the other to talk first. After a sigh, Maizie blurted out the question she wanted answered so badly. She blinked her big doe-eyes in his direction, "Does this mean I can finally get in your room to clean?"

Hearing her caustic tone, he swallowed down the mouthful of shake his tongue was savoring. "Tomorrow morning you can get in there and go at it." Then he narrowed his eyes at her, "But only if you tell me why no one will stay in that room?"

Her face split with a full smile. "Promise you won't freak out on me." The straw still in his mouth, he nodded. "Besides the usual number thirteen bullshit, it was also the room that I found the dead cat's blood in the bed."

He nearly dropped the tall shake glass he was holding, "The What?!"

She laughed at his initial reaction but calmed his fears by telling him the story of her scary discovery of the bloody room. Then along with how the police determined it was a ritual that included killing a cat. She rounded the story off by saying the police found the lunatic that performed it and locked him in a mental institution.

While she told the story he examined her face, noticing the subtle features of another race. Which one it was, he wasn't sure. Could be Native Indian or Mongolian. Whatever she was, her lustrous black hair and big brown eyes captivated him as she spoke. When she laughed, her face lit up with delighted joy. It had been too long since he spent time with someone so cheery — and so naturally beautiful.

She ended the tale with a reassuring, "But don't worry. We threw the bloody mattress out and got a new one."

He laughed out, "That's good to know."

She noticed how his sapphire eyes lit up when he laughed. She also took a quick glance at his scraggly beard and wondered what he would look like without it. 'Handsome gentleman,' she told herself. And a good haircut would put him right on the cover of any men's fashion magazine.

They sat quiet, the same nervous tension between them. Gabriel, careful not to say too much — Maizie, too anxious to speak. Thankfully the awkwardness was broken when Maggie showed up with his meal. "There you go." Like the pro she was, she gently placed the plate in front of him, the gravy-laden hot turkey sandwich to his left. "Ketchup?"

"Yuk. No."

"Suit yourself." She looked at Maizie's plate and snapped, "Done now?"

"No," she barked back.

"Fine. Either of you need anything else?"

Both shook their heads no. Gabriel already had his mouth full of mashed potato and gravy.

Maizie noticed how the gravy glistened on his lips. 'Sexy ... kissable,' she thought.

He chewed twice and moaned, "This is good. That's real turkey."

His excited moan went to her ears, then traveled downward, settling in between her legs. She squirmed in her seat as she picked at her plate, as she knew she would.

He was too busy eating to notice — or talk, so Maizie filled in the conversation. "You sound like you haven't eaten all day."

Through a mouthful of stuffing, he mumbled, "That's true. I haven't eaten since the other night."

"Last night?"

He shook his head NO.

"I knocked on your door last night too. But you didn't answer."

"I was asleep." His expression turned to one of self-preservation, "Why? What's the big deal if I didn't answer?"

"Nothing. I just wanted to clean your room." She stuffed a chunk of cold carrot in her mouth.

He kept his eyes on the roasted turkey he was cutting with his knife but aimed the question right at her. "You really got a thing for cleaning my room, don't you?"

She shrugged, "It's my job."

"Tomorrow." He stuffed the turkey in his mouth, "Tomorrow, you can clean it all you want." He witnessed the disappointment in her eyes. "I've been mostly sleeping, so the room isn't that dirty."

"The bedding needs to be changed and the bathroom has to be cleaned." She pushed her plate away, "If the health board comes in and inspects, I'm in big trouble."

"You mean, Gord is in big trouble."

"Which trickles down. Meaning, I'm in trouble with him."

He scraped up the last of his potatoes and used the loaded fork to make his point. "But I would tell the inspector that I'm the reason you couldn't do your job."

Maggie poked the coffee pot between them, "More Maizie?"

He took note of the housekeeper's name, tucking it in his memory for later.

She put her hand over top of her mug, "No. Too many and I don't sleep."

She didn't ask about his shake, "How's the hot turkey?"

He swallowed down a big mouthful to answer her, "Good. Real good. What kinda pie do you have?"

She went down the list of flavors. He stopped her at lemon meringue and asked her to make it ala mode with chocolate ice cream. "You got it, Hun. Be right back."

Maizie finally put her mug and silverware on top of her plate. "You staying much longer?"

Gabriel had been so guarded for so long, he automatically answered with a question, "Why do you want to know?"

Seeing his eyes narrow slightly, she kept her reply light and friendly. "Just curious." Feeling as though she was interfering in his life, she excused herself from the booth with a brief, "Have a good night," and headed to the cash register. But no sounds came from the till. She simply signed her bill and handed it back to Maggie. Maizie took one last look at the handsome yet secretive stranger sitting in her booth, then left out the open door. The others inside yelling to close it quick, the cold wind was coming in.

When his pie came, Maggie took away both plates, "You need anything else?" her tone was doubtful, knowing there was no way he could possibly eat another damn thing.

"Nope, this is good. Just the check, please."

"You mean bill." When he didn't understand, she explained, "It's not a check, it's a bill. Why people get that frigged up, beats me." She stomped away, not waiting for his excuses.

Gabriel ate the ice cream and as much of the pie as he could, his stomach aching at being overstuffed. He stood by the front till waiting for Maggie to come out of the kitchen.

"All done?" From her apron pocket, she pulled out his bill and entered it into the register. "That'll be ..."

She didn't get to finish. He shoved a twenty and a five across the counter, "This should cover it. Keep the rest for a tip."

"Wow. That's mighty generous. Thank you." It had been a long time since she received a five-dollar tip.

THE LAST MOTEL

He simply nodded and left. From where she stood, she watched the man walk down the street, his red and white plastic bag flung over his shoulder as though he didn't have a care in the world. But her wise-women gut told her different. From what Maizie had told her about the man, and his unkempt appearance, that man was running from something.

SIX

Further down the sidewalk Maizie waited, pretending to window shop in the hardware store. She was waiting for Gabriel to reach her so she could strike up another conversation. His answers were guarded in the restaurant, maybe if she talked to him alone, he would open up to her.

Gabriel scanned the streets for the two thugs —they were either not in town or well-hidden out of sight. That's when he saw her waiting ahead. He kept his stride the same so she didn't think he was hesitant about running into her. He also knew what was coming once he reached her. She was going to ask him more questions he didn't want to answer. Through suspicious eyes, he pondered if he should trust her. Or worse, put her in danger by telling her what he knew — what Heather knew. What Heather was murdered for. No, he couldn't tell her that. In his mind, he quickly categorized what information he could tell her and what would save her life when Rene and Cash came for him.

"Hello," she greeted him, using her friendliest smile. She fell in beside him, matching his lumbering pace. "Feeling better?"

He rubbed his stomach, "Feeling stuffed … and tired again." He saw her face fall. "Don't worry. When you knock on my door in the morning, I'll be ready for you. Promise."

Maizie didn't trust promises. Men promised her lots of things, then never did them. "We'll see," was all she snapped back.

Her hostile reaction made him glance in her direction. Seeing her tight lips and set jaw, he instantly understood her sharp reply. The woman walking with him had been mistreated by someone — most likely some man with ulterior motives. Pretty women like her probably had guys lie to them constantly, disappointing them with every scam. He stopped and looked directly into her face, "Tell you what. You can start with my room first. What time do you want me up?"

A soft grin lit up her face, "You don't have to do that."

"Nine o'clock? Ten?"

Realizing he would not give up, she offered a time that worked with her schedule, "Ten is fine." She started walking, him falling in step with her. When they had reached the corner, Maizie stopped. "I'm going down to the river. You wanna come along?" She was praying he would join her. She hadn't got all the information on him yet and she wanted more details. Trying to convince him, she blurted out, "It's beautiful this time of year. Fall colors and no bugs."

He raised an eyebrow, not believing her, "No bugs?"

Maizie's caramel colored cheeks blushed pink, "Okay, okay. Not as many as in summertime." As though a child, she lowered her head, hiding her guilty face from him.

He laughed at her confession. Feeling bad for teasing her, he agreed to keep her company. "That sounds good. Besides, I could use some fresh air." He swept his hand in front of them, "Lead the way."

She headed down the side street, talking over her shoulder. "It ain't fancy but if we're lucky, we might see some deer or maybe a bear."

Gabriel stopped dead in his tracks, "Bear!"

"Black bears. Rare, but it happens."

Ahead of them was a mowed patch of grass that held a set of swings with an attached slide. Off to one side, sat a few wooden picnic tables. Maizie headed straight for the one right out in the open. "Sunshine's warmer," she explained her choice. "If it ever comes out, that is." She plunked down on what he noticed to be a very ample rear end and swung her feet over the bench part to facing the river. She patted the long seat beside her, "Sit here."

"Yes, boss," he joked.

Again, she blushed. She felt the need to clarify her advice. She pointed with her chin, "So you're facing the river ..."

"Figured that." After he scanned his surroundings for his two assassins, he slid in beside her, leaving a respectable amount of space between them. Neither one spoke as they took in the scenery. Small ripples of white formed around the rocks that protruded the river's surface, telling Gabriel that the water ran faster than it appeared. The tall grass had begun to turn brown and every other tree was transforming to some shade of gold, brown or red. Fall was definitely setting in.

"There." Her hand slowly pointed towards the far upper bank. "Fox. By the biggest rock."

Gabriel stretched his neck, "Got it." They both stared intently at the one spot. "He's beautiful," he whispered.

"He's a female."

He chuckled, "And how can you tell that from here?"

"Smaller ... brownish rather than red." She turned to face him, her face a witty smirk, "... and no nuts." That made him roar out loud. "Shhh!" she scolded.

He clamped his hand over his mouth. "Oops. Sorry."

She pointed again, "There. Beside the tall grass. Three kits."

"Kits?"

"Baby fox," she stated matter-of-fact.

"Oh." He watched them dart to the water's edge, take a drink, then dash back to the protection of the tall grass. Gabriel understood how they felt. That's exactly what he was doing himself — hiding for protection from two predators. Rene and Cash were always there on his mind. They could show up anywhere, anytime, ready to kill him on sight. As much as he wanted to relax, he could never completely let his guard down.

When the mother joined the kits, they began to play fight, the smaller one getting the better of the larger two. When it swatted a paw, connecting with the head of the biggest, toppling him into the water, they both laughed out loud. Four heads turned in their direction, lowered, and froze. As fast as they had come, they disappeared, slipping back into the thickets.

The sun broke through the clouds. Feeling the warmth on his skin, Gabriel closed his eyes and leaned his head back. He felt his muscles relax slightly. One by one the knots eased. The turkey from his dinner along with her company added to his sudden desire to nap right where he was.

Seeing his eyes closed, she took the opportunity to secretly scan his face. She admired his physique as well. Thick thighs combined with square muscular shoulders — her favorite body type. Again, her groin reacted to him being so close to her. Picking at the wooden surface of the picnic table, she casually asked one of the questions she wanted answered, "So you're a salesman. What exactly do you sell?"

'Damn it,' he swore in his head. He hadn't thought that far ahead. With no readymade lie, he said the first thing that came to mind. "Well, I kinda lied about that. I'm currently ... shall we say ... between jobs."

"Oh?"

"Yah. Last boss was a real asshole and I had all I could take of his bullshit." He stretched out his legs and crossed them under the table, "When I got my last paycheck, I told him to shove it."

"Okay. But what WERE you doing?"

He turned to look at her, "Curious one, aren't you?" The breeze caught her scent and wafted it in Gabriel's direction. 'Sweet almonds,' he noted.

She didn't like his tone, so she lightened the mood with a joke. "Yep. 'Curious One' is my middle name. Third generation ... on my mother's side."

He smiled with half his mouth.

"Sorry. It's a game I play. You know ... what does the guest in room 13 do for a living?"

"Besides killing cats?"

It was her turn to chuckle at his wit. "You don't look like a cat killer."

His forehead frowned serious at her, "So what does a cat killer look like?"

Through a laugh, "They wear three-piece suits and drive green sports cars."

"Green sports cars?"

"Yah. Ugliest thing I'd ever seen. And I've seen some really ugly cars."

"Can't say I've ever seen a green sports car."

She turned to face him, her blouse opening up enough for Gabriel to get a glimpse of her cleavage, "Even in the city?"

Surprised by her question, he raised an eyebrow in her direction, "I never said I was from the city."

"Well, with that soft pale skin of yours, you ain't from around here." She flipped her long black hair over her shoulder, "Cheap sneakers, no boots. License plate code isn't from this district either." She reached over and twisted his hand, palm up, "And your hands don't exactly look rough from working hard in the mines or bush."

He was astonished at how much she knew about him without him saying a word. "Jesus. You picked up all that? You a PI in your spare time?"

She grinned wide at his complimentary joke. "No. I've been in this business long enough that I've learned to read people. And I'm right about 90 percent of the time."

That made him curious, "Yah. So what did I do before this?"

Turning to face him, she batted her lashes, "I don't know. You keep skirting the question."

"Got me there." He stood up, stepping over the seat. "Getting late ... and all that turkey is making me sleepy again." He stopped, turned to her still sitting at the picnic table, again scanning the area around them. His own need to stay safe spilled out of his mouth, "You need me to walk you back? Or are you okay on your own?"

She laughed hard, "Like I need your protection now that you're here." She swung her legs over the seat, "Been walking these streets alone for over three years and now YOU want to protect me?"

"Point taken." He still waited until she reached where he stood.

She walked by him; him falling in step with her. She faced forward while she asked again, "Not going to answer my question, are you?"

"Sorry, no." In his head he answered her, 'I'm running from two mobsters that want me dead. And the less you know, little lady, the better.'

When they reached the street, the topic switched to the nearby businesses and local characters that lived in the small town on the edge of nowhere. He constantly searched the streets and alleyways, praying the two men weren't hiding in wait for him. He didn't want Maizie to be caught up in his horror. He had already planned to run the other way if they showed up, pulling them away from the innocent Maizie. The knot in his gut was back again — tight and hard as ever. He forced himself to listen to her melodic voice, hoping it would calm his anxieties. And for the most part, it did.

She talked of everyday people living everyday lives in a small town. What would seem mundane to many city people, sounded like heaven to Gabriel. Especially if he could spend it listening to her soft voice. Had he been alone for so long that he became starry-eyed towards the first woman he encountered? He made himself keep his distance from her — and the tiny hand he wanted to hold. To feel the warm flesh of another human being was tempting. A simple hug from her slim arms would melt him where he stood. But inside he knew he shouldn't start something he couldn't go through with. In two days, he would be gone, and anything he started with her, would only cause her great pain afterward.

~

Back at the motel, Gabriel excused himself, politely stating that he needed to see Gord. When she tried to come with him, he said no, saying he needed to talk to him in private. A guy thing, he explained.

She shrugged and went on her way, back to her room. She noticed the blue pickup was still gone. She couldn't remember how many days the man had booked a room. Dallas was a rare name in Northern Ontario, marking him as another outsider. With a shrug she closed the door to her room behind her, wishing her and Gabriel's evening together had lasted longer than it did.

~

Hearing the office door open, Gord looked through the door leading to his apartment to see who it was. He reluctantly got up from his recliner and shuffled into the main office. "You're back?"

"Yep. Good eats at Kathi's Kitchen." Gord agreed with a nod. "I ended up sitting with Maizie. I came for my keys."

Gord's jaw clenched at the thought of Maizie spending time with another man. Particularly a man that was hiding from someone. His chivalry told him he had to protect Maizie from Gabriel. He picked the keys up off his desk and slid them across the counter but kept his hand over them. Their eyes connected. "So what kind of trouble are you in anyway?"

The question was asked in a tone that told Gabriel he wasn't getting out of that office without answering him. He inhaled deeply and gave Gord enough information to satisfy his curiosity. "I saw someone killed and the murderers are after me."

Gord's jaw dropped in shock — then set hard again. "And you're bringing them here to MY MOTEL?" his last two words furious.

Gabriel held out halting hands, trying to calm him down, "Hold on, hold on. I lost them in Wawa."

"Bullshit!" he was about to yell at Gabriel again but the man cut him off.

"I took the highway running north. Followed some lumber side roads to throw them off." Gabriel leaned forward, trying to look directly into his eyes. But Gord, feeling threatened, took two steps back. "When I got here that night, there were no headlights in my mirror. I'm telling you, I lost them." He inhaled deep again, trying to ease the pressure in his chest. "Besides, I won't be around much longer. Two days tops."

That seemed to appease Gord. "Sooner would be better." He threw the keys at Gabriel, hitting him in the chest. "I don't want any trouble."

"And I don't want it here either. I swear."

Gord blew anger out his nostrils, trying to control the urge to hit the man that brought danger to his peaceful little world. "So what do these guys look like?" He crossed his arms and sat back on the edge of his desk, "Just in case they come looking for you."

Gabriel shuffled his feet, debating whether he should tell him or not. But he knew he had no choice. Besides, better he knew, that way Gord could be his warning system. "The leader of the two is Rene. A real prick. Sold his mother out to the cops so he could get the Crime Stoppers cash. Then he used it to open a storefront that sold drugs to high school kids. A real dirt bag." He leaned against the counter, his elbows supporting his tense body. "The other is called Cash. Have no idea why ... just is. And like Rene, he's one sick bastard. Heard he chopped up a guy in Medicine Hat for not paying his drug money. The kid was robbed. They took everything. Cash didn't care and killed the boy to show others that he accepted no excuses. Enjoys using a machete he carries around with him."

Gord's face soured, "And they are coming here for you?" He crossed his legs, "Good thing we hid your car." An image of his Maizie flashed in Gord's mind. He needed to make sure she was safe.

"But they have no idea where I am. And they don't even know what car I'm driving." His face flushed red, "I kinda swapped it out."

"Wow, you've thought of everything." So that's why Gabriel paid cash, instead of a credit card — not traceable. He tilted his head and squinted at him, "So now, the question I have is ... should I trust you?"

Gabriel was afraid that would happen. "Yes, you can." He stood up tall and squared his shoulders, "Look, I don't want anything to happen to you or Maizie. Or anyone else in town for that matter. If they come around, I'll run for it, making sure they see me, drawing them away from you and the motel." He crossed his chest with his finger, "I promise."

Promises didn't impress Gord. Too many people, mostly women, gave him promises they never meant to keep. He examined Gabriel's face. Behind all the scraggly facial hair, he searched for the truth. "You involved in drugs?" Gabriel immediately shook his head that he wasn't. Gord dropped his folded arms, "You still haven't told me what they look like. Details ... I need details."

Gabriel blew out the breath he'd been holding. "Rene is five-foot-ten. Balding with a black hair halo. Slim but don't let that fool you. He's wiry as hell. Hard runner too."

"And this Cash?"

"All muscle. Six-foot-one. Blonde ponytail, white mustache. Wears a black leather coat. Knee length to hide his machete." Gabriel swiped his finger down his right cheek, "And a scar that starts at his temple and ends on his chin. A gift from his brother apparently."

Gord stood silent, studying the stranger in front of him, wondering if he should believe him and let him stay — or kick his ass out of his motel.

Nervous that he was about to be told to leave, he pulled the roll of bills from his pocket, "I'll pay extra if you let me stay. Two more days, then I'll never bother you again." He held up a single hand in oath, "I give you my word."

Calmly, Gord scrutinized Gabriel again. As the seconds went by, Gabriel's face slipped into a pleading expression. Yet Gord's gut talked to him, telling him that the man needed a safe haven, if only for those two days. He stood up from the desk, "Put that away. You've already paid me too much. Starting to feel guilty about it too." Then he pointed at Gabriel, "But in two days, I want your ass out of here. I've got my Maizie and the others to worry about."

Gabriel's heart exploded with relief. "Thank you" He held out two fingers, "In two days, I'll be gone. That's a promise."

"Yah, yah, Get out of here. My cop shows coming on and if I miss the first five minutes, the rest of the show don't make sense. Now scram!"

Gabriel was so relieved, he almost danced out of the office. "Thanks, man. You won't regret it."

As he watched Gabriel walk back to his room, Gord was sure of two things.

One, he would indeed regret his decision.

And two — trouble was on its way.

SEVEN

A loud bang outside his motel room woke Gabriel. He shot straight up in bed, looking around to see if they were there in his room. Whether he had to grab his backpack and run again. Nothing but darkness and quiet surrounded him. He slumped back onto the bed and let out his held breath. He pulled the covers up to his chin and closed his eyes tight. His post-adrenalin emotions overwhelmed him. What time was it? He turned to read the red numbers on the bedside alarm clock — they glowed 2:13 AM. He covered his eyes with his arm again, blocking out the same red glow.

His heart rate was elevated and his fight-or-flight instinct had kicked in. That urge for him to leave, to run away into the darkness, was strong. Was he about to have another flashback or would it pass him by? He tapped his fingers on his chin to distract his mind like the old man had said to do. "You are safe," he told himself in a whispered voice. "Relax. Breathe." He was relieved when no images flashed through his mind and continued the technique the soldier had taught him to make sure they didn't. He continued to tap and breathe purposely, focusing on both sensations until the impulse to escape left him. But once gone, that need of flight was replaced with another sinister emotion he had not been able to evade so easily.

The darkness of despair.

A despair so deep, it ached in his bones.

Wearing him down as the night went on.

As much as the evening with Maizie had been enjoyable, he had also noticed that he couldn't completely relax while in her company. Always looking over his shoulder to see if Rene or Cash was lurking in the background, waiting to get him away from the others to murder him. Or more likely, one clean shot to the head before they disappeared without a trace.

He knew they would always be there, hunting him, being their defenseless prey.

It was that cold hard reality that had brought on his latest bout of despair. The depressing knowledge of his future. A life of continuously being on the run, lurking in the shadows for his assigned huntsmen. Ceaselessly worried that they would find him in a vulnerable position and shoot to kill.

That's the way it had been for weeks. Him running, only stopping to rest when he was ahead of them. So exhausted, his body and mind giving out. But they would find him again and try their best to eliminate him without getting caught in the act. They were relentless with their mission, dogging him down highways, through cities and small towns.

Up until that point, he had managed to outrun them, outsmart them by guessing their next move before they themselves had thought of it. They were getting smarter, making themselves less visible. They were doing what he had been doing, anticipating his next steps. But how much longer could this go on before they found him again? How much longer before he would have to grab his backpack and escape out the window or back door?

Even after three days rest, he was still tired — still exhausted, both mentally and physically.

He wasn't sure how much longer he could keep running. Or if he even wanted to any longer. What was the point of running? Two brains for predicting and tag team driving while the other slept. They always found him. Besides, he had nothing left.

Heather, the love of his life, was gone.

The life he once had with her was no more.

His future was empty — with no purpose.

There was no hope.

"So why go on?" he asked himself, the words hung hard in the dark.

He was simply tired of running. Tired of worrying if the next corner he turned down would be his last. He also worried about collateral damage. Who they would kill to get at him? Just as he was the target to eliminate as the witness in Heather's murder.

He was starting to believe it would be better if he did the deed himself, saving innocent bystanders from being in the way of their bullets.

He lay in the bed, thinking that it was the best solution. The only solution.

To take his own life. To be done with it.

The pressure in his chest was heavy, crushing, smothering his breathing. The decision was dark — darker than he had ever let his thoughts slide before. Once he allowed himself to slip fully into his depression, the strategies came quickly. He would do it soon, saving everyone in the motel from Rene and Cash's bullets.

But how to accomplish it was the decision he had yet to make.

Pills? He had no medication, so that method of suicide was out.

Bleach? His body shuttered at the thought of the pain the clear liquid would cause to his throat and insides. No. He wanted to die, just not in a painful way.

Hanging was next in his thoughts. Question was — how and with what? He pulled his arm off his eyes, looking at the light fixture above him in the dim light. It was of no use. It was a cheap fixture, probably from the local hardware store. Two light bulbs above a round of mottled glass. It would rip out of the ceiling before it held his weight; only giving him bad rope burn instead of death.

His arm back over his eyes, he racked his brain for another solution. He remembered Heather reading an article on how a local teen had hung himself using a belt stuck in his closet door. He didn't own a belt but he was sure he could get one at Stedmans. If not, a rope from the hardware store would do the trick. Nylon. Something with no give. He rolled over on his side, curled up, holding his legs with his arms. The shift in position caused the heaviness in his chest to hurt more, the sharp spikes shot into his ribs then into his back. He was so mentally drained he didn't even have the strength to groan about the stabbing pain. Instead, he slowly inhaled and held his breath, waiting for them to subside. The pounding in his ears throbbed faster, demanding that he take in air for oxygen. He didn't want to. He just wanted to die. He wanted it all over with. To slip off into darkness, never having to worry another second about the two goons trying to murder him.

'I should let them kill me. Death by assassin,' he thought. But he knew that was not the answer. His and Heather's death would be for nothing if that happened. He needed to do it his way to ensure the truth got out. The truth of what Heather discovered about their local mall and the ring the mob ran out of the food court.

That's why he had been running. To keep that information from being destroyed by the two hired guns. He let out the air in his lungs, taking in a deep breath to stop his heart from pulsating overtime. He couldn't kill himself yet, he had to expose the evidence Heather had collected.

He needed to transcribe Heather's notes onto sheets of paper. Then photocopy them, making enough copies that he would mail them off to people he knew would take action on what Heather documented. To do something about what was happening in plain view of everyone at the mall. Until that was done, he would have to hold off on ending his misery

He had to finish what Heather started.

Another deep breath, slowly letting it out. Fatigue was taking over, shutting his brain down to the emptiness. He needed to sleep.

Sleep his only escape from his hopeless life.

~

Being woken by the sound of a vehicle door slamming, Maizie lay in her bed, her mind still fuzzy from the dream she was pulled out of. The man with the pickup in room 2 was back. She ran a hand over her face, smiling at the craziness of the images in her dream. They were of her and Gabriel walking in a field, holding hands and laughing. They were a couple in love. She felt heat rush between her legs as her mind recalled what they did on the plaid blanket he laid out for them. She could almost feel the dream — the sun feeling warm on her naked skin as he made love to her.

A dream she hoped would come true before he left.

She had never felt this way about any man that had stayed at the motel. Mainly, she avoided their creepy advances and offers of twenty-dollars for 'a good time.' She simply reminded them that housekeepers were not hookers. And if they persisted, management would kick their rude asses out.

Maybe that's what attracted her to Gabriel. The fact that he treated her with respect. Like a true lady. It also helped that Gabriel was a sexy looking man. At least he would be after a proper shave and haircut. She would hint at that tomorrow while cleaning his room. Her bedside clock read 2:25 AM — she would see him in seven and half hours. She had so many questions, but mostly she couldn't wait to be around him.

She rolled over on her side, forcing her mind to restart the dream again. Right where they left off before the truck door woke her. The smile on her lips laxed as she drifted off to sleep again. The image in her mind swirled into a dream of her in his arms, his mouth on hers, tender and passionate.

~

Jolted awake, Gord stood up in his office, looking out the windows in all directions. When he saw nothing but the man locking his truck door and returning to room 2, he laid the rifle back on top his desk. He had been keeping watch since midnight. Sitting at his desk, his best automatic hunting rifle across the arms of his chair, prepared to shoot anyone that threatened those staying at his motel — especially his Maizie. He took another drink of his coffee to stay awake. Stone cold.

He shuffled to the coffee maker to make a fresh pot. According to the wall clock, it was only 2:16 AM and that meant it was going to be a long night. If Rene and Cash were coming to kill Mr. Smith, he was ready to protect the people that lived at The Last Motel. He didn't give a damn about the man in room 13. Cash could gut him with his machete as far as he was concerned. It was the others he cared about. Crazy old Tula and the even older Moses — those two he would protect.

And then there was his Maizie. He stood by his desk, sipping coffee, and looking out the large picture window towards the door of her room. He knew deep down in his heart, he was willing to lay down his life for her. He couldn't bear the thought of not having her in his life. He would rather be dead than live without her.

The man in the pickup came back outside and lit up a cigarette. His sat in the round chair Gord had provided for every room. A beer bottle dangled from his other hand. Gord chuckled at the image. Before him sat a man with no cares in his world. Relaxing with a smoke and a beer. 'That's the life,' thought Gord. "Someday," he whispered to himself. He scanned the parking lot and street one last time, then sat back down behind the desk — one hand on his coffee, the other on the rifle resting in his lap, ready for whatever the night would bring.

~

Wind blew cigarette smoke into Dallas's eye, making it sting and tear up. He wiped away the tears with the back of his hand before chugging down the last of his beer. Out of boredom, he peeled off the label of his Molson's Canadian, laughing that he would get 'lucky' because it came off in one piece. Another chilling wind blew down his neck, making him shiver. He ground his cigarette butt into the cement with the heel of his boot and stood to go inside. He took one last look out at the street, wondering if tomorrow he would spot the man he had spent all day looking for. Driving up and down the highways and back roads.

THE LAST MOTEL

Gabriel Carr was somewhere in Northern Ontario, and if he found him first, he would be the one to get the thousand-dollar reward offered by the Davol Brothers. He went inside, closing the door on the cold wind and darkness of the night.

EIGHT

Maizie took her time fixing her braid, pulling the crossed tufts slightly to make them seem fuller. She wished her hair wasn't so straight — or so black. She flittered her bangs with her fingertips, once again considering the idea of dying her hair chestnut brown or perhaps a dark blonde. Any color that made her look less like her Inuit self. But that would have to wait for another day. Right then she was too busy getting herself ready to go clean Gabriel's room. She had gotten up early so she could take a thorough shower, making herself 'fresh' in case things heated up in his room. She grinned to herself in the mirror at the possibility of having sex with the stranger. Next to complete was her makeup. She applied just enough to enhance her looks, yet not enough to look 'made up.' A little blush, some mascara and a layer of cherry red lip gloss. She skipped her normal eyeliner and bronzer — thinking that would look over the top.

Luckily for her, the Dallas dude had left a message with Gord that he didn't want his room entered so her workload for the day would be light — and fast. Checking the time, 9:53 AM, she zipped up her uniform top, smoothing down the front with her hands, feeling her breasts under the ugly grey fabric. Her nipples instantly reacted to her touch, hardening into small sensitive nubs. Yes, she was a woman with needs. And if things worked out, she would be sharing her bed with Gabriel soon. She was so excited, she nearly danced on tiptoes, at the thought of spending time with Gabriel again. That's when she stopped herself in front of the mirror. She talked to her reflection, her face stern. "What are YOU doing?" she asked herself in a whisper, as though someone might hear her. She was trying to rationalize her strong feelings about the man and the situation. "He's just a city guy passing through. Are you sure you want to do this?" It took all of two seconds for her to laugh at her reflection and yell, "Hell, yes!" with a fist pump. She herself was amazed at how fast her feelings for the stranger had escalated in such a short period of time. She made her way to the laundry room to get her cleaning cart. Then she headed straight to room 13 and the waiting Gabriel.

~

As Gord always did, he waited by the big picture window that looked out towards the motel's courtyard. Each morning he would watch Maizie leave her room to retrieve her cleaning cart from the room next to hers. It was part of his voyeuristic spying that made his day more bearable. To secretly enjoy watching her from a distance — her being innocent and unguarded. But what he noticed that morning didn't make him happy. Maizie was 'gussied up.' Wearing makeup on the job? She never wore makeup at work. In fact, he couldn't remember the last time Maizie had worn makeup, period. He also noted the spring in her step and the way she pushed the cart, her chest pushed out, making her breasts look round and pert. When she bypassed Moses and Tula's room, going straight to room 13, Gord's mouth fell open with worry. Was she going to Gabriel's room to clean — or to fool around on him.

When she turned the corner to head down the right side of the courtyard, Gord also noticed that her hair was done differently. When she stopped in front of room 13 and rubbed her hands down her uniform, over her luscious body, he nearly lost it. "God Damn it," he cursed under his breath. He quickly knocked on the window, reminding her that he was still there, waiting for her to love him.

~

Reaching the door of room 13, she stopped the cart and automatically checked herself over. She checked that her braid draped down the right of her chest, out of the way but still curved to enhance the fullness of her breasts. She ran her hands over the uniform again, feeling the same female sensations as before. Then she wondered if it would feel that good when Gabriel's hands did it. And she wanted him to do it. She licked her lips to make them wet and glossy, kissable. She heard a tapping sound coming from the direction of the office. She looked up to see Gord knocking on the window, waving good morning to her. She waved back, smiling at his friendliness, then turned back to face the door. Maizie's hand hesitated midair before she knocked, her nerves rattled at the possibility of Gabriel kissing her. No answer. While waiting, she turned around to look over the courtyard. She noticed that the blue Ford truck was still gone.

The door quickly opened in front of her.

Gabriel stood in the doorway, wrapped only in a sheet from the waist down. "Sorry. I slept in ... I guess."

~

Gord's hands formed fists at his side. Anger forced his heart rate to pound in his ears. The nerve of that city asshole, meeting his Maizie half-naked. When she happily pushed the cart inside and closed the door behind her, his heart shattered into a million miserable pieces. The sharp pain in his chest crushed his lungs. He took two steps back and sat on the edge of his desk, trying to catch his breath. "Maizie ... don't do it," he whispered. "Oh, my Maizie ... don't."

~

Gabriel hastily covered the top half of his body with the dangling section of the sheet. His cheeks flushed, "Um, sorry. Let me get dressed." He grabbed a handful of clothes off the dresser and waved them, "Bathroom." In three long strides, he closed the bathroom door behind him.

Maizie laughed at his bashful nature. Yet she was happy to be able to see what Mr. Smith had been hiding under his black t-shirt. She also noticed that he looked dreadful. Dark circles under his eyes made his face appear tired. There were subtle signs that he might even be depressed. Not a good time to bother him about getting a decent haircut and shave. Setting herself to work, she started with making the bed. She stripped off the bedspread and tossed it in the laundry bag hanging from the cart. There in the middle of the bed was a backpack, military green, and plain, no pockets. She was about to pick it up when Gabriel yelled from the doorway of the bathroom.

"Don't touch that!" He stormed right to where she was and scooped it up off the bed, his fist white tight on its top. He stomped by her, "Excuse me."

Maizie clutched her hands to her chest, getting them out of his way. She stayed where she was, wondering what the backpack contained to make him react in such a harsh manner. Drugs? A gun? Whatever it was, he was protective of it, clutching it tight against his body.

Seeing her frightened expression, he felt bad for his actions and changed his demeanor — and the subject. "I've never done this before." He swirled his finger in the air, encompassing the room, "Do you want me to stay in here while you clean ... or should I go outside and wait?"

She smiled at his question, "You can do whatever you want to do." She pulled off the bottom sheet and tossed it in the cart. "But if you stay inside, keep out of my way." It came out harsher than she meant it to be.

He half-saluted her, "Yes, ma'am," then sat in the only chair in the room. "This good? Ma'am?"

She nodded as she laughed at his playful teasing. However, inside, she felt she had blown their rendezvous already. "I just don't want to hurt you. That's all." Next, she took out the clean sheets and began making the bed. She snapped the first flat sheet out over the mattress and began tucking in the corners and sides.

Gabriel watched her work, enjoying the mastery of how the housekeeper did her job so efficiently. He also noticed Maizie's ass as she bent over to tuck in the corners. Maizie had one of those bodies that made men crazy. Slender legs, round rear end, trim waist and breasts that looked like they felt soft and sexy. By the time she pulled the bedspread in place, Gabriel had to stop his groin from reacting to the unintentional show performed by Maizie the housekeeper. He held the green backpack in his lap, hiding the bulge that was threatening to form in his jeans.

Seeing his discomfort, Maizie gently asked, "Are you okay?"

"Yah, just tired. Didn't sleep too good last night." Oddly, he found himself somewhat happy to see her again. Just to have her in his presence made him feel less — lonely. Even with their scant conversation, he could feel himself perk up. And that feeling was the complete opposite of the despair he had suffered in the darkness the night before.

Going from one extreme to the other was confusing him. The emotional flip-flop of going from last night's hopelessness to his current contentment, tugged at his heart — and his groin. His primal reaction posed a question in his mind. Were the emotions running through his body because of her specifically, or could they have been brought on by any female that came into his lonely life? Either way, the tension between them was unmistakable. Boy wanted girl and girl wanted boy.

"Me neither. That guy with the pickup truck needs to stop slamming his damn door." She was lifting the vacuum cleaner off the cart, the action making her breasts heave upward in the low zippered cleavage of her uniform. A spectacle Gabriel's eyes enjoyed immensely. Vacuum on the carpet, she gestured toward the bed. With a voice half sultry and half commanding, she gave her orders, "Gabriel ... get on the bed." The confused expression on Gabriel's face told her he was unsure why she had asked him to get on the bed. She let the sinful thought linger between them, teasing at both their sexual appetites.

He smiled at her, his blue eyes twinkling his hunger for the feel of human flesh. For hot reckless sex. He could almost taste her pleasure on his tongue — the softness of her full breasts in his palms.

She could have easily seduced him right there and then. Her right hand twitched at her side. One zip down her uniform front and he would have been treated to the sight of her sexiest bra. The red lace cupping each aroused breast into mounds of soft wanting flesh. But she lost her nerve, not going through with what her heated crotch was begging her to do. "So I don't hit your feet with the vacuum," she explained.

His lustful expression fell flat.

He walked to the bed and lay on his side, leaning on his elbow so he could continue to watch Maizie's body as she cleaned. The backpack he coolly tucked behind him, out of her view but where he could feel it against his back.

He watched her as she vacuumed, taking in each stroke of the vacuum on the carpet. When she bent over to vacuum the baseboards, he had to look away to stop an erection he couldn't exactly hide where he lay.

She gingerly returned the vacuum to the cart and picked up a red bucket filled with cleaning supplies. She stole a glance in his direction, taking in his relaxed body. His jeans snugged his muscular thighs. She noted that the black t-shirt he wore, clung to every muscle in his taut torso. She turned away quickly before she could no longer restrain herself. In her head, she knew she did not want to seduce him there in his room. It would feel cheap — like a sleazy act a hooker would perform for drug money.

And knowing he needed to calm the heat between them, he changed the subject to something more mundane. Luckily, his stomach grumbled at that moment, giving him another reason to talk to her. "Say, do you know a good place for lunch? Someplace that serves really good poutine."

"Yah. The Royal." She stopped at the bathroom door, "They use real cheese curd and home-made gravy. Nothing chemical." Then she disappeared from his view.

He listened to the sounds of her cleaning, his mind imagining her bent over, her round ass teasing him in his mind. He forced himself to sit up and behave. She was at work. Not there to provide a free show. He ran his hands over his face, bringing himself back to reality. When she backed out of the bathroom, he asked her straight out, "Since I have no idea where The Royal is ... would you like to come with me?"

She put the bucket on the cart and picked up her dusting rag. "I'd like that. But it's too early, they don't open until noon." She shook the rag, "And I have to finish my work."

"Later then. When you're done."

She blushed slightly, "But that won't be until at least one o'clock." She started dusting down the TV.

He tried not to watch her ass wiggling back and forth in front of him. "That's fine with me. Give me a chance to do my shopping first."

Maizie stopped what she was doing to look at him, her finger sarcastically pointing downward, "Shopping? In this town?"

"Yep. Stedmans and the hardware store." A puzzled look came over her face. "Guy stuff."

"Oh."

He felt the need to explain further, "Some more clothes, bug spray, and a big flashlight. You know ... guy stuff."

She stopped her dusting, "Okay, sounds good. Meet me in front of my room at one o'clock."

"Can we walk there ... or do we need a taxi?"

Again, her finger pointed mockingly downward, "In this town? A taxi?! HA!" She leaned over and dusted under the bedside table — a place that didn't really need dusting. She arched just right, showing off her best features, Her cleavage level with Gabriel's eyes. "Besides, it'll take all of twelve minutes to walk there. A nice stroll if the winds stay down."

"So it's a date then?" He chastised himself for using that particular word, 'Date? Stupid move, dumbass!'

Maizie tossed her dusting cloth on her cart. She kept her voice as calm and casual as possible, "Yah, like I said ... sounds good." She took one last look around, checking to make sure she had done everything she was supposed to. "Okay, all done here. I'll see you at one o'clock." She nodded towards the door, "Can you get that for me?"

"Oh yah, sure. Sorry."

She laughed at him, "You apologize too much." She noticed the backpack on the bed, realizing he had been hiding it behind his back the whole time. She would have to ask him about it at lunch.

"Well, that's 'cause I mess up a lot," he joked back.

With the cart outside, Maizie waved her goodbyes and pushed it down the room fronts, making sure her ass wiggled in an enticing manner.

Gabriel in turn, watched her ass walk away for a few moments, then returned inside the room, closing the door behind him. He slowly felt the joy leave the room — leaving his life. He felt the emptiness return. The same despair that had haunted his night once again seeped into his soul. Rene and Cash were not going to go away. They would still be dogging him until they found him and killed him. He heaved a sigh and sat on the edge of the bed, his body slumped with futility. He knew inside that his decision to end it all, was the best solution.

He got up and dressed for the outdoors, stuffing his wallet in his back pocket. He was about to open the door when he remembered he had one last task. To hide his backpack. He wedged it between the back of the small desk and the wall. He would have to find a better place to hide it — and its important contents — Heather's notebook.

~

The next room she wanted to visit belonged to old Moses. Cleaning his room wasn't on the schedule but Maizie had noticed lately that his room had needed extra attention, particularly the bathroom. She was worried that maybe Moses was having health problems. She knocked on his door loudly so he could hear it over the TV. She waited, hearing him move about inside. He slowly opened the door a crack then let her inside.

"Morning Moses." Her smile wide, her voice cheery, "How are we doing today?"

"We? What's this WE bullshit?" Obviously, he was in one of his cranky moods again. "I'm God damned tired. Don't know how the hell YOU are ... and why would I?" He huffed as he made his way to his favorite chair, "Young people ask such stupid questions."

She pushed her cart inside, "Oh Moses, you know what I meant." She was so happy about her lunch date with Gabriel even miserable Moses couldn't dampen her spirits. She ignored him and did a quick dusting.

"And why are you here anyway? It's not my day."

She was surprised he remembered the weekly schedule. Instead of telling him the truth as to why she was there, she used her news as the reason. "To be honest, I'm killing time." Her face beamed as she told him of her afternoon plans. "I have a date."

That tidbit of information perked Moses up. "Oh yah. Who's the lucky guy?"

"Gabriel."

His eyebrows popped up in shock, his question more disbelief than surprise. "The new guy in 13?" He made a disgusted face, "Kinda scruffy for my taste."

Maizie laughed, "So you're into men that are snappy dressers, are you?" That got her a sour look from the old man. She made her way to the bathroom and as she had suspected, it was a mess again. But this time the turquoise bowl was speckled with both brown and red dots. She walked back out to talk directly to the man who made that mess. She sat down on the edge of his bed, bringing her eye level with his, "Moses ... I'm concerned about you. Lately, your bathroom has been ... shall we say, unhealthy."

He narrowed his eyes at her, not attempting to dance around the unpleasant subject, "You mean ... shitty."

She blushed at his bluntness, "Yes, that."

He raised his chin, keeping his dignity. "Well if you'd stop showing up off schedule, I would have had it cleaned up before you came in."

Her mouth dropped open with alarm, "Are you telling me that you have been cleaning that up before I come into clean?" He nodded rapidly, his face flushing scarlet with embarrassment at being caught. She reached out to touch his boney knee, her words filled with sympathy, "Oh Moses, I had no idea."

He pushed her hand away and looked straight ahead, avoiding her pitying eyes. "Oh don't feel sorry for me. I'm fine. Doc says it's nothing to be worried about. It'll clear up in no time." He right out lied to her. The doctor told him he had six months, nine at the most, before he would have to find a nurse to take care of him in his final days. Bitter about his situation, he waved her away, "Just leave the ... mess. I'll clean it myself."

Maizie knew Moses well enough that there was more to the story. "No, I'll do it. It's my job." She stood, "And I'll add your room to my daily list."

"NO!" he shouted.

She didn't understand, "Why not?"

His face tensed anxiously as he reluctantly explained, his words almost a whisper. "Because I don't want Gord to find out. He'll kick me out ... and then I'll have to move to one of those nursing homes." His fists clenched and his forehead furrowed, "Death traps ... all of them."

Maizie then understood why he had been hiding it from her. She patted his knee again, "Don't you worry, Moses. Your secret is safe with me." She stood up, giving him a fond peck on the cheek, "You are now on my daily schedule. And if Gord says anything, I'll tell him you're teaching me Spanish."

His face screwed up, "But I don't speak Spanish."

"Neither does Gord! So how will he ever know!" she roared. His face split with a big grin at getting a prank by Gord. She was happy to see a smile returned to his face. "Okay, I need to get your bathroom done pronto ... or I'll miss my date."

As she cleaned, he quizzed her about her upcoming rendezvous. "So this Gabriel guy, you stuck on him or is this a quick roll in the sack."

"Moses!" she squealed from inside the bathroom.

He laughed hard, then stopped quickly before he made another mess in his adult diaper.

"Honestly, I don't know where it's going. Nor do I care. If it's just sex, that's fine. If he sticks around, that's good too." She remained quiet, concentrating on her cleaning, trying her best to not contaminate herself in the process.

Moses considered Maizie as a daughter, wanting only the best for her. "Are you sure about this Maiz? Seems like you're setting yourself up for disappointment."

Admiring the sparkling turquoise bowl and seat, she left the bathroom and tossed the soiled rubber gloves on the cart. She sat across from him again, "Moses, I'm not so lonely that I'd do something that was not in my best interest."

Her statement of self-protection seemed to satisfy his fatherly concerns. "Then I say ... go for it." He slapped the arm of his chair and bellowed, "Fuck him 'til your legs hurt."

She roared again, "Oh Moses. You dirty old man." She walked to her cart. "Like I said. I'm not sure where this is going. I'm just letting it happen." She shoved the cart out the door, "I'll see you tomorrow. And no cleaning up before I get here ... Señor!" She stuck out her tongue and closed the door, both of them chuckling as it clicked.

She was worried about the old man. She planned to talk to Doc Sanders about his condition. With patient confidentiality, he may not tell her anything but at least she'll know she tried.

On his way downtown, Gabriel made a list in his head of the things he needed to buy. A pad of paper and a leather belt from Stedmans. A ten-foot piece of nylon rope from Home Hardware and a can of bug spray to protect himself against the last of summer's pests that were, at that moment, eating him alive as he walked.

Each step was a conflict. On one hand, he was thrilled to have lunch with Maizie. A happy occasion filled with excitement and sexual tension. But the same steps were also filled with a cold hard reality. He was on his way to buy the items he would use to take his own life. To end the misery he had been living for months. He pulled up his coat collar against the wind blowing directly in his face and he told himself, "Two days." He dug his fists into his coat pockets as a sign of his determination, "... and this will all be over."

NINE

From inside the office, Gord's eyes were trained on Moses's door. Maizie had left room 13 and went straight to Moses's room. It wasn't the old man's day for housekeeping services — so why was she in there? Frustrated, he ran his hand through his hair. Hair he was ready to pull out because of what he feared was happening between his Maizie and the city guy, Gabriel. He paced the width of the office again, the knots in his gut getting tighter and harder. When he saw the cart emerge from the old man's room, he wanted desperately to run across the courtyard to talk to Maizie. But that's exactly what it would look like — an act of desperation. To control his agitation, he shoved his hands in his pockets, "Settle down. She's still here. And Mr. Smith ain't." He started to pace again, his mind filling itself with unseen images that could have happened behind the door of room 13. Did they kiss? Did he persuade his innocent Maizie into having sex with him? "Slick talking city bastard!" he growled between clenched teeth.

He watched as Maizie pushed her cart down the front of the rooms, then park it while she opened the laundry room door. She looked good. Her hair in a fancy braid, not its usual loose ponytail. And her make up brought out her facial features, the ones that first attracted him to her that day in Sault Ste Marie. When he had seen her under the park bench — asleep, her eyes closed, her face angelic. A purity that triggered his need to protect her, to save her from herself. To love her. He had lost his heart to her even before he had offered her the housekeeping job at his motel. When she didn't accept his offer straight away, he was sure he had wasted his time. He could still remember looking up from his desk when the door opened and her standing in the doorway, her face a mixture of smiling fear. It was all he could do to not jump over the counter and hold her tight, reassuring her that he was going to take care of her forever.

But that was three years ago — and long before Mr. Smith showed up.

He watched her go to her own room, closing her door without looking his way once.

"Her Room ..." he mumbled out loud.

That was his answer!

He'd spend the money on two — no three rooms, so she could redecorate them. That would make her happy. Make her want to stay with him and not leave with Gabriel Asshole Smith. It would take all his money but if she stayed and loved him back, it would be worth it.

~

At his first stop, Stedmans, Gabriel headed straight for the rack of bug repellant, grabbing a spray can for his chrome wire basket. Next went in a pad of lined writing paper, followed by a package of envelopes he hadn't thought about when he made his list. His lunch with Maizie was weighing on his mind. Had he made a mistake inviting her along with him? He knew the word 'date' was a massive error but he would straighten that out with Maizie while at the restaurant. He casually made his way to the men's department — all six racks and four shelves of it. He stopped at the belt rack and picked out the longest one, dark brown with a punched pattern in it. He looped it and placed it on top of the other items and continued to look around the small department store. Most of the clothing was meant for local working men. Farmers, lumbermen, and those that worked at the mine north of town. It was a sea of workwear green and dark denim. The outer sleeve of a bottle blue shirt caught his eye amongst the dull colors. He held it up, checking its style. Instantly, he felt a distant memory pull at him. It was Heather's sultry voice telling him 'blue is so your color. It makes your eyes irresistibly sexy.' His lips remembered the kiss that followed her words. The tender lovemaking on the living room carpet.

The mere thought of her sparked his memory —
The memory of her murder.
It exploded in his head.
Images rushing through his terror-stricken brain.

Heather's laughing face in the soft morning sunlight.

The sound of the gun.

Heather frozen while red chunks burst from the back of her head.

Her body sliding to the ground.

Then nothing — the flashback was gone.

Only his crippling emotions remained with him, paralyzing him in place. He hung onto the shelf for balance as he waited for the episode to subside. He tapped his fingertips on the side of his leg to focus his swirling thoughts.

Slowly the sounds in the store returned, no longer overpowered by the rushing blood buzzing in his ears.

He hung the blue shirt back up and took the white one next to it, throwing it into the basket. He pretended to look at other items on the shelf, waiting until his legs were ready to move. He had endured hundreds of flashbacks since Heather's murder, most mild like the one he had just experienced. Others incapacitating — vivid and violent, bringing him to his knees with heart wrenched pain mixed petrified fear.

"Hello. You need some help over there?" the sales lady yelled over a stack of boxes she was pricing. Her face beamed wide, "Find the size you're looking for? Got some in the back, if you need a certain size."

He inhaled slow and deep to calm his racing heart. "I'm good, thanks. Just looking."

She eyed the city guy up and down before returning to her ticket gun, "Suit yourself. Happy to help if you need it. Just holler."

Gabriel grabbed his basket and retreated to the back of the store. He spent several minutes gathering himself together before having to meet the chirpy woman at the checkout. His depression made other 'happy' people unbearable to be around. He needed more time for his emotions to settle before facing someone who was currently humming along with the radio. "Flashlight ..." he reminded himself. Finding it two shelves over, he added it to the wire basket that was increasingly pinching the palm of his hands.

With a bubbly smile, she asked that annoying question all salesclerks ask, "Find what you were looking for?"

Gabriel just nodded and emptied his merchandise on the counter.

"Good to hear." She punched in the prices but stopped at the belt. "This is way too big for you. Let me get you the right size."

She was halfway around the counter before Gabriel stopped her, "No, I want an extra-long one."

Her face screwed up with curiosity, "What for?"

His brain blurted out, "It's to hold a suitcase together. Lock's broke." He distorted his expression to look embarrassed, "Cheaper than buying a new one, right?"

"Makes sense." She rung it in and bagged it all up. She was pleased he paid in cash. So many paid by credit card and those companies took two percent of the sales, meaning she made even less profit. She handed him his change and his bag, "There you go. You have yourself a great day." Gabriel simply nodded back and left the store, relieved to be away from such a cheery person.

Outside, he forced his legs to walk forward. The minor flashback had hit him harder than he thought. He inhaled the cool fresh air deeply, trying to lessen the tightness in his chest and stomach. He was on his way to buy the one item he knew he would use to kill himself. A rope that he could tie around his neck to strangle himself lifeless.

A rope that would end all his dark suffering.

He no longer wanted to feel the pain in his heart for the loss of his girlfriend.

Death would be a relief.

~

In front of the rack holding the rolls of chain and rope, Gabriel shifted his red shopping bag from one hand to the other, freeing up his right hand. He rubbed his thumb along the surface of the ropes that he thought would work. The first cord was too thin, probably unable to hold his weight, snapping before it cut off his breathing and blood supply. The second, felt rough to his fingertips. But what did that matter if he was going to die from it. On the bottom of the rack, half-hid behind a full roll of chain, was what he was looking for. Finger thick yellow nylon rope that he was sure would do the trick. 'Trick,' he laughed in his head at the choice of word. Then he stopped laughing, gloominess replacing his grin, 'Some trick? Dangling from its end … lifeless and disgusting.'

Wanting a length of that rope cut, he looked throughout the store. The only sales clerk available was talking to another man, his face tense, and his voice terse but low enough that it was meant to be a private conversation. "I told you before Moose, I can't give you credit."

"But why? You know I'm good for it," the man begged with his hands.

"That's not the issue here." He shoved past him, "It's not allowed. Head office will get pissed off. And I simply can't afford to have them mad at me again." He turned back and looked at Moose over the top of his black-framed glasses. "You are NOT worth me losing my store over."

He offered with a crooked grin and a shrug, "So ... don't tell them."

"It don't work that way. I have to put everything through their inventory system."

"So, don't put it through."

"Okay." He looked him in the eye, making sure he would understand, "You're not hearing me, Moose. I'm NOT going to do anything." His hand went on his hip, telling the man he had made up his mind. "The answer is NO. And NO again."

"But I need the parts today." He was pleading with the clerk, his hands knotted in front of him. "Without it, I can't finish the job. And that means no paycheck." He rubbed his flat hand over his mouth, "Roxy's gonna kill me if that happens."

"Sorry, Moose. Them's the rules." He pointed to the sign on the wall. It read 'NO CREDIT' in big red letters.

"Damn you, Allan!" he stormed to the glass door and grabbed the handle, ready to open it. "Fuck you, Allan! See if I buy another damn thing from you. You cheap son of a bitch." He yanked the door open and disappeared out into the windy day.

Allan just shook his head and laughed. Seeing Gabriel looking in his direction, he explained why he found it all so funny. "We're the only hardware store in over a hundred miles. Trust me, he'll be back. Probably dragging his no-account whore of a wife and their three dumb-as-shit kids behind him." He took a few steps toward Gabriel, "You need some help with something?"

With the spew of poisonous words from his mouth, Gabriel didn't want the man to serve him. He had the feeling half the town would know he bought a piece of rope by that evening. "No. I'm just looking."

"You're new. Where you from?" Allan walked towards Gabriel, "And why are you here in this shithole town?" When Gabriel didn't answer him, it prompted him to ask more questions. "You from the mines? Worker or inspector?"

Gabriel just nodded, not answering any of his questions. But the closer Allan got to Gabriel, the faster panic rushed through him. The clerk's in-your-face insistence triggered another attack of emotional instability inside Gabriel. He skirted by Allan and headed straight for the door, blurting out his excuse, "Forgot the measurements. I'll come back."

"You do that." He stood and watched Gabriel leave, wondering who the unfriendly man was. He'd have to ask around as to who the bearded stranger was.

Gabriel heard the phone ring inside the store as he was walking away. He let out the breath he was holding and started to tap. Two fingers on the outside of his thigh, his mind concentrating on each time his fingertip made contact with the material of his jeans. He breathed fresh air in through his nose and let it rush out his mouth. He was sure he was doing it backward, but at that moment, it was working and that was all that mattered. He was almost at the motel when his need to escape calmed down so he could breathe normal, his heart not wanting to explode in his chest. Disappointed that he had failed to get the most important thing on his list, he resolved to go back to the hardware store after he had lunch with Maizie. A lunch he wasn't sure he wanted to go on after his wretched shopping trip. His hands were still shaking when he tried to unlock his door. Inside, a quick peek at his wrist told him he still had time to call their lunch date off. He'd give himself another ten minutes to collect himself. If he felt better after that, he would go with her and enjoy a fine lunch of poutine.

~

The office door stayed open while slow-motion Moses made his way inside. "Morning, Gord." He walked to the little table and poured himself a coffee, black. He eyed the last two muffins on the cardboard tray. He picked up the biggest one and pointed to the other, "You gonna eat that last one?"

Gord, in no mood for the old man's games, snapped at him. "No. Take it."

Moses wrapped them individually and stuffed them in his pockets. He took a sip of his hot coffee, wincing at how hot it was on his sensitive chemo mouth. He watched Gord's finger-twisting a yellow pencil as though he wanted to kill it. "You okay Gord? You kinda look ... agitated."

Gord slapped the pencil down with a loud SNAP! Scaring Moses so much he jumped, spilling coffee on the floor. He quickly wiped his cotton slipper over it, sopping up any evidence. He blew over his cup, waiting to see if Gord was going to talk about what was bothering him or not. Not getting a response, he poked the bear. "You mad at someone, Gord?"

He shot the old man a dirty look, "Yes, I'm mad at someone." Then he paused, thinking it was better to not admit he was angry at Maizie. Moses was a bigger gossip than Tula, so what he said would get back to everyone by the end of the day. "Well, not mad ... just concerned."

"Oh? About who?" He slurped off the rim of his hot coffee.

"Maizie." He was about to tell him why, but the senior interrupted him.

His face lit up at spreading Maizie's news. "Oh, you don't have to worry about her. She's going on a date for lunch."

Not revealing that his statement had wounded him inside, Gord tried to keep his voice casual. "Oh yah ... with who?"

Moses pointed with the same hand that was holding his coffee, "The guy in 13. Damned excited about it too."

Gord's heart cracked in two right where he stood.

"I told her I didn't care for the man myself." He took another sip. "Too unkept for my liking."

Gord turned his back on Moses, hiding the tears that were forming in his eyes. He swallowed hard to remove the lump in his throat. "Yah, I'll be glad when he's gone."

Moses reassured Gord, "Don't worry ... I warned Maizie to be careful with a city guy like him. They're fast in the city. Having sex at the drop of a hat."

Gord clenched his fists below the counter where Moses couldn't see them. "But they're just going for lunch. What can happen at lunch?" Somewhat under control, he loosened one hand and wiped away the last of his tears with his fingers. "Besides, it's Maizie. She's a good girl. She wouldn't do something like that."

Moses laughed out loud. "Not according to her. I think she's hoping he'll try to get her in bed." Moses felt his insides shift, telling him he needed to hurry back to his room. He raised his cup, "Well, thanks for the breakfast." Without hesitation he left the office and headed straight for his door, praying he'd make it to his bathroom before soiling his diaper.

Sitting at his desk, Gord was fuming. She wanted him to hit on her. She wanted him to take her to his bed. She was throwing herself at him. "YOU WHORE!" he screamed seconds before clearing off the top of his desk with his arm. Paperwork flew in all directions, while everything else crashed to the floor. His breath heaving, he drove his fists into his thighs, hammering until it hurt more than his heart did. He bellowed to the ceiling, "Why, Maizie? Aren't

I good enough for you?" He stepped up to the filing cabinets and with both arms, cleared their tops off too. "Slut! Piece of trash! I should have left you in the dirt where I found you." He placed his hand on the cabinet tops, ready to fling them to the floor when a movement outside caught his eye. Gabriel was returning from his trip to town. The red bag clutched in his hand, his feet almost on a run.

Had he seen Gord's outburst in his office?

Embarrassed by the thinking that Gabriel may have witnessed his ugly behavior, Gord immediately pulled himself together. What was he thinking — it was a business office. What if a new client had walked in the doors at that moment? "Get a grip ..." he scolded himself. With his jaw set hard to control his remaining rage, he frantically picked up the paperwork and files that were strewn all over the floor. When all was returned to its original place, sort of, he sat down in his chair. His hands trembled as he picked up the same yellow pencil and strangled it again. This time pretending it was the man in room 13.

~

Tula slowly closed the gap in her avocado curtains. She shook her head in disbelief at what she had witnessed. Gord had thrown an adult size temper tantrum inside his office. Whatever Moses had said to Gord, it made him angry enough to trash his own desk. She slowly laid down on the bed, her feet tucked under the turned down bedspread for warmth. She planned to talk to both Gord and Moses to get the details on what happened to make Gord act like a raging brat. Laying on her bed, he sighed deeply before she wriggled her frail body into the blankets for comfort. But not until after she'd had her customary afternoon nap.

Youth was so wasted on the young.

TEN

Thirty-five minutes. Gabriel had that amount of time left to get himself together before his 'date' with Maizie. Besides his stomach aching hunger, he had decided to not disappoint her and go on the 'date' after all. Even though he felt exhausted, he didn't dare have a nap, fearing he would sleep through his alarm like he had that morning. Flashbacks always did that to him, draining all his energy, leaving him weak, both physically and mentally. But there wasn't time. He needed to wash off the stress sweat that had coated his body during his flashback. He grabbed the backpack from behind the dresser and headed for the bathroom.

Hot water streamed over his muscles, relaxing their tension. He closed his eyes, making himself concentrate on his upcoming lunch with Maizie; doing his best to suppress the emotional baggage from his earlier trauma. He forced his thoughts to those of gravy-laden poutine and cold beer. He hoped they used real cheese curd as Maizie alleged they did. Grated mozzarella cheese was an insult to the legendary Canadian cuisine. His stomach growled again when he bent over to dry his legs. At the sink, he dried his hair with a hand towel. Combing his hair in the mirror, his hand still shook slightly.

Looking at his reflection, he wondered where the old Gabriel had gone. He had lost at least twenty pounds, his ribs visible through his skin. His face had changed too. Under his scruffy beard, he could see his sunken cheeks and pale skin. Dark circles under his eyes added to the look of a man that was not taking care of himself. "Food. You need food," he told himself, "... and more sleep."

But the sleep he desired was not for rejuvenation — it was for escaping the darkness that had taken him over. A method he used to avoid the depression that had sunk into his soul, refusing to leave.

For Gabriel, his life was empty.

Pointless.

There was nothing to look forward to.

No plans to make.

No one to make the plans for or with.

Except for one.

In two days he would complete his fatal plan, making his unbearable despair go away. As odd as it was, his upcoming suicide made him feel lightweight — the beginning of his unburdening. The darkness would end and he would be free. He decided that he would do his best to enjoy his lunch of greasy poutine and cold beer with the motel's housekeeper.

Also to thoroughly enjoy his last two days on earth.

He dressed in his new shirt and the dark jeans he wore before. Part of him was excited to meet up with Maizie — part of him was not. After the flashback in Stedmans, he still felt rattled, once again unnerved by the brief images that haunted him. How could he simply bury his feelings about Heather, the love of his life? But he would have to if he was to enjoy his time spent with Maizie. The red numbers on his alarm clock read, 12:47. Maizie expected him at one o'clock. Pulling on his socks, his legs felt like they weighed a ton from all the stress he was under to perform. To portray himself as a happy-go-lucky guy from the city. Yet, he was fully aware his afternoon could also be upbeat. But only if he permitted himself to feel that way. If he pushed down the heartache and the fear, he could enjoy her company.

Maizie — and poutine. Good company and good food that any man would be happy to take pleasure in. He just had to push past the sad darkness and allow himself those indulgences.

His last job before leaving to meet Maizie was to place the writing paper and envelopes in his backpack, shoving it behind the dresser out of sight. Knowing what pests waited for him outside, he liberally sprayed himself with the bug repellent to keep the little bastards from biting his neck and any other exposed skin.

At the door, he calmed his nerves and put on a fake grin, ready to meet Maizie at her door. He was going to have fun with his date — even if it killed him.

~

Maizie looked at herself one more time in the mirror. She liked what she saw. Her reflection made up more than before, but still natural rather than glamorous. And her tight red sweater looked much better than the ugly grey uniform Gord made her wear. This time she let her long hair loose, the braid from earlier giving it slight waves. Any kind of texture in her straight native hair was welcome. She just wished she had taken the time to curl it. She shrugged, "It'll have to do." She checked the clock on the wall in her mini-kitchen, 1:00 PM. She wondered if she should wait inside for Gabriel or meet him outside. She peeked out the sheers and spotted him locking his door, jiggling the handle to make sure his door was indeed locked. Her heart skipped with delight. She couldn't wait for him to knock on her door, she needed to be with him immediately. She slipped on her windbreaker and grabbed her purse. Unlike Gabriel, she didn't worry about her door being locked. She had nothing worth stealing. Which made her wonder what Gabriel owned that made him so determined to lock up his door tight to protect. As far she could recall, the only possession in the room was the backpack he hid behind him on the bed. What was in the backpack that was so important? Another question she needed an answer to.

He arrived just as Maizie exited her door. He greeted her, his phony smile in place, "Hey. You ready to go?"

She inhaled deeply, bracing her self-confidence, then grinned widely, "Yes. Yes, I am."

He kept his hands in his jacket pockets, not only to keep them warm against the wind but to avoid any awkwardness of her attempting to hold his hand. "You look nice."

The compliment excited her so much, she skipped a step, "Thanks."

"And you smell good," she complimented in return.

They were halfway across the courtyard when he realized what she was referring to. He laughed, "Yes, it's my new cologne ... Eau de deet."

It took her a few moments to get his joke, then laughed loudly, her hand flirtatiously swatting at his arm. "You're very funny."

"Yah ... and that ain't the first time I've been called funny." When she reacted in the same flirty manner, he decided to change the subject to one that allowed her to talk — and him to not talk. "So besides poutine, what else does this restaurant serve?"

"Oh, lots of wonderful things. They have ..."

And off she went, telling Gabriel the menu, item by item. Gabriel simply nodded like he was paying attention, only listening when she said the name of a dish that piqued his interest.

~

Inside the office Gord watched Gabriel meet Maizie outside her room. Moses was right, she was going on a date with the stranger. He stood frozen while Maizie slapped Gabriel's arm. A flirty move if there ever was one. His heart fell to the pit of his stomach. "Maizie ... don't go," he whispered at the window's glass. He couldn't watch it anymore. He turned away, focusing his attention on the silver bell sitting on the counter. He walked to it, leaning his elbows on either side of it, talking to his tiny curved reflection in its dome. "Gord, my boy, you gotta step up your game before that city slicker gets your Maizie." In his view, Maizie and Gabriel walked by the front window, Maizie talking a mile a minute, Gabriel nodding with a stupid grin plastered on his face. Maizie spotting Gord inside, waved at him, then returned to her conversation as though he was invisible.

By the time they disappeared beyond the window frame and out of Gord's sight, his temper hit an all new high. He grasped the bell tightly in his hand and threw it. It hit the wall with a CLANG, bouncing backwards across the floor in a vein of chinking sounds. Before it had stopped its racket, Gord turned around and cleared off his desk again, all the items crashing against the metal filing cabinets. "Bitch!" He sat down hard in his chair, his nostrils flared. His fists pounded its plastic arms, "I hate you!" His face distorted with an angry scowl, "You WILL pay for this." He hammered his thighs, "I'll make your life a living hell ... WHORE!" The sound of Dallas's truck driving into his motel parking space pulled him out of his fury.

Gord watched the peculiar man through the window, wondering what he was doing with the red duffle bag. A narrow-snubbed duffle bag that was obviously not meant for hockey equipment. When Dallas turned towards the office, Gord ducked behind the wall so he didn't see him spying but nearly slipped on his metal stapler. Once he

126

caught his balance, he watched the reflection in the window of the room across the court. Much to his horror, it reflected that Dallas was walking his way. Gord sank to the floor and began to gather things, tossing them up on to his desk as he went.

When Dallas entered the office, all he could see was items being thrown up in the air, landing on the desktop. As he got closer to the counter, he found Gord on his knees, stacking papers neatly on the floor. "Hello."

Gord's red face tilted up, "Hey." He continued to gather the files, tapping them on their end to square them up. "What can I do for you?"

Dallas squashed his urge to ask why the office had been trashed, thinking he didn't want to add someone else's problem to his own long list of bullshit. "Looks like I'm staying for another couple of days." He slid his credit card over to Gord.

Feeling the heat of his reddened face, Gord attempted to explain the office's chaos before reaching the counter. "Wind caught hold of everything and whoosh, down it went."

Dallas said nothing, keeping his face still.

The man's rigid composure made Gord uneasy. "Um, yah. Two days." Except the card was different than the one he used previously. Gord read the name — Grigor Dallas Borisov. 'Russian,' was the first word that popped into Gord's mind. While he processed the card, he wondered what a Russian was doing in his motel. "So, what are you doing around here that's making you stay another two days?" He regretted the question the second it left his mouth.

Dallas's expression went from tranquil to threatening in a half-second, "No one's business." He crossed his arms, telling the nosy man to not ask any more annoying questions. The duffle hung from his hand, dangling like a red warning sign to shut his mouth.

Gord shoved the finished paperwork at him, "There you go."

He signed it, took his copy and folded it in half. He stuck it, along with the credit card into the unzipped side pocket of his duffle bag. He turned and left without a word.

The cold wind from the open door sent another chill over Gord's already goose-bumped skin.

What Gord saw inside that unfastened pocket, scared the hell out of him. Inside sat a box of ammunition. But it wasn't your run of the mill hunting ammunition. They were 54mm bullets with pointed tips. Ones that were made for high power rifles, created specifically to kill from a long distance. Sniper bullets. Gord's guts flip-flopped and tied themselves in a colossal knot. "Holy shit ..."

Dallas was an assassin — and Russian.

~

As the gentleman he was, Gabriel held out Maizie's chair. "Thank you." She blushed at being treated so regally.

The hostess waited until Gabriel had seated himself fully, "The waitress will be with you shortly. Enjoy your evening." It was said routinely, with no emotion or friendliness. She left them sitting together, both feeling awkward at the table. it held three lit candles and a tiny bouquet of miniature roses in its center.

It immediately registered in Gabriel's mind that the restaurant was not what he had expected. It was a romantic dining establishment, not another greasy spoon like Kathi's Kitchen. The walls were faux red leather created by the trendy paint technique. They had used metal studs to create a pattern, enhancing the dark brown moldings that encased every baseboard, and corner. The look was dark and heavy, bringing Gabriel's mood down again.

A waitress showed up, her uniform designed to not hide any of her assets. The hem high and the neckline low. "Good evening. My name is Twyla and I'll be your server for the night. Oops, sorry, this afternoon." She blushed as she continued her rehearsed dialogue. "Today's specials are fresh trout with wild rice and buttered vegetables. Also, we have a mushroom quiche with tossed green salad. And lastly, prime rib with sautéed mushrooms, your choice of potato, and buttered vegetables." She laid the menus in front of them, being careful to place them the right way up — not like she had done no more than twenty minutes earlier at another table. "I'll give you some time to look the menu over." She visually scanned them over, determining if they would leave her a good tip or leave nothing like the rest of the cheapskates in town. "And could I interest you in a beverage with your dinner?" She knew she had said it wrong again but didn't bother to correct herself. The afternoons were not her regular shift.

But extra money was always welcome. The more she saved, the faster she could get out of the shit-hole town.

Gabriel grinned up at her, "I'll have a Canadian."

Maizie didn't like the way he was looking at the waitress. He was HER date, not fair game for the waitress to hit on. "I want red wine," she ordered just a little too sharply, getting a perplexed look from Gabriel.

Twyla wrote down their orders, then disappeared, leaving them alone again.

"Wonder what else they have?" For safety, he opened up the tacky looking menu, focusing on it rather than Maizie. She was watching him too closely for her to not consider this lunch an actual date. He decided to keep the conversation light — friendly, rather than intimate. "Have you eaten here before? Any recommendations?"

She opened up her menu, looking for the same dish she had ordered the last time she was there. When she first came to work for Gord, he took her there for dinner several times. Unfortunately, they had changed the menu since last spring, the dishes she had enjoyed were no longer listed. "Yes, I've been here before. But everything has changed." She spotted what she wanted but the price was outrageous. There was no way in hell lamb chops were worth twenty dollars a plate. She closed it and laid it on the edge of the table. She immediately wanted to wash her hands after handling the grimy plastic menu. That meant going to the lady's room and she was not about to leave Gabriel alone with Twyla. "I'm going for the trout. I know they get it in fresh daily, so it should be good."

Gabriel stacked his on top of hers, "I'm going for the prime rib …"

At that moment, the drinks arrived, Maizie nearly gulping down half her wine to wet her dry nervous throat.

She stood ready with pen poised over her pad. "So, have you decided?" As required, Twyla took the woman's order first. To control her lazy eye, she looked downwards into Maizie's face, aiming her wonky eye along the side of her nose, securing it in the center of her eye socket. "And what can we get you this evening?"

Maizie glanced up and was shocked by the waitress's uppity attitude. Who was she to look down her nose at Maizie? To show her who was boss, she straightened her back and with a cool tone, ordered the trout. Gabriel's expression once again asking why she was being rude in that way. To show him she was relaxed, she placed her elbows on the table and rested her chin on her hands. They quickly turned into tightened fists. Her date with Gabriel was not going the way she had planned.

And it was all Twyla's fault.

Her breast nearly pushing out the top of her dress. And the back hem barely covered her ass, exposing Twyla's legs. Long legs that Maizie didn't have.

"And you, sir?" Her head held in the same position, her eye centered.

He smiled sweetly at her, hoping his charms would influence her into agreeing. "I'll have the prime rib, but instead of the sides offered, can I substitute poutine instead? Or can you at least go into the kitchen to ask the chef if he could?"

Maizie did not like that grin. Was he really flirting with the waitress in front of her? And on their date no less. She gritted her teeth while she waited for Gabriel to be finished ogling the waitress.

Since it had been a slow lunch crowd that day, she knew the guys in the kitchen would have no problem switching the order. She smiled widely, "I'm sure we can accommodate you." She picked up the menus. "But we'll have to charge you a little extra. Is that okay?"

He nodded, "No problem. I'm too famished to argue."

With a sharp nod, Twyla made her way to the kitchen.

Maizie huffed out, "Wow, what a bitch?"

Maizie's comment shocked him. In his opinion, Twyla had done nothing wrong. But not wanting to spend his afternoon listening about why the waitress was a bitch, Gabriel changed the subject completely. He relied on his old icebreaker, "So, tell me Maizie, what do you do for fun?"

Her head tilted, "What do you mean?"

"When you're not working, what do you do for fun?"

She panicked inside. Truth was, she didn't do anything exciting enough to talk about. The only thing she did in her spare time was work on her plans for the motel renovations. "Not much. Mostly work on my proposals for Gord." She could see he was waiting for more information. "You see, I have a plan to rejuvenate 'The Last Motel.' I want to bring it into the twentieth century. Do away with all the old ugly avocado green and harvest gold décor."

"And the turquoise toilets?"

"Yes, those monstrosities too," she smiled that he was actually listening to her. Unlike Gord who just nodded every now and then. She continued with the details of her renovation ideas. Nervous, she kept her eyes focused on the one finger that was rubbing the rim of her wine glass. "Once all that's in place, we can start to offer packages to hunters and honeymooners. Romantic packages that include chocolates, flowers, and champagne ... luxuries to set the mood. Hunters would get meal coupons for Kathi's Kitchen. Or at Karl's Keg House for a night of cheap drinking. Half price pitchers and discounted wings by the pound. That type of thing."

"Wow, you really have thought it all through."

"I have." Her face brooded, "Now if I could only get Gord to do it."

"He hasn't gone for the idea? Can't see why. Your plans sound wonderful. Innovative and forward thinking for such a small town."

"That's the problem with Gord. He's old, so he thinks old. He's not young like you and me. He has no adventure in him. No desire to stir things up. Try new things." She looked directly into his eyes and licked her lips, "You should come to my place ... to look at my sketches." She left a pause on purpose, to emphasize her next sentence, "Then you'd see how adventurous I can be."

By the expression on her face and the sultriness in her voice, Gabriel knew what she was hinting at. A place he wasn't ready to go. He would have to stop her advances before they went too far. "Maizie, I think ..."

Much to Maizie's irritation, Twyla showed up with their dinners. "Here we go. Trout for the lady. And for you sir, prime rib with poutine. By the way, the chef laughed when I put in the order. He said he liked your style." Noticing Maizie's wine glass empty, "Another for the lady?"

Maizie nodded, her jaw set tight with annoyance.

Gabriel raised his beer, "Me too." Twyla was barely gone before Gabriel was stuffing his mouth full of poutine. He moaned at the richness of the gravy. The squeakiness of the fresh curd against his teeth and the crispness of the French fries. Gabriel was in culinary heaven.

Maizie, still watching the waitress walk away, narrowed her eyes at Twyla's back. Twyla was ruining everything. Gabriel was about to tell her something but she interrupted him. Her eyes narrowed with hate for the woman.

"You're right, this place is awesome. How's your trout?"

She quickly took a bite to please him. "Delicious. Very fresh and moist." One taste, and she too, found herself eating rather than talking. The two ate in silence except for the occasional approving moan from Gabriel. Those manly moans turned Maizie on. Each one humming from his lips, landing in her ears, surging down between her legs. Her need for him was growing faster than she could handle. She took a deep breath to slow down her racing heart. She was even happy that Twyla had shown up with their drinks, placing them on the table without a word.

Gabriel drained his first beer. "This is perfect. Just what I needed." Into his grinning mouth went another forkful of poutine.

With his mouth full, Maizie started up the conversation again. "So, Gabriel, what do you do for fun?"

He laughed at her using his own clever question on him. "I'm a writer. Well, trying to be one." She nodded that she was listening. "Although I haven't written a word since I've been on the ... road." He almost said 'run,' and that would have been disastrous.

"Anything published?

"No. Not yet." His use of the word 'yet' surprised him. He would be dead tomorrow night. There was no 'yet' — there was nothing. There was no Heather. His face slipped to a frown with the thoughts of his miserable life and his plans to end it.

Maizie, seeing what she thought was disappointment from not being published, reached across the table, and held his hand. It was the opportunity she was hoping for. A reason to touch him, to let him know she cared about him and that she was willing to go further if he wanted to.

He felt Maizie's warm hand slip over his. He looked at her hand, her's dark against his pale hand. When he raised his eyes, looking directly into hers, he saw her true intent. She was offering more than comfort. There was no mistaking the fact that she was offering herself to him.

"Are you okay? You're so sad."

Staring back at her hand on top of his, he felt a distant recollection of skin-on-skin. However, he wasn't feeling Maizie's flesh.

He was reliving the memory of Heather's body against his.

Her soft lips on his.

His hands upon her silky body.

Their lovemaking.

The sweet smell of her hair as they slept together afterward.

But Heather was dead. And he would never feel her again. His broken heart crushed in his chest, making it impossible to breathe. Maizie's thumb moved, bringing him back to reality. To get himself under control, he inhaled deeply, letting it release slowly through his nose.

He knew he needed to stop Maizie from what she was doing. For fear it would insult her, he didn't pull his hand away immediately as he knew he should. Instead, he let it linger as if she was merely comforting him. "It's just writer's remorse. We all want to be published and fabulously famous. And then there's the money." He pulled a forkful of poutine upward, making sure the curd was stretching a long string from it. He took his hand away from Maizie's and pinched it off, half wrapping it around the tines of his fork. He quickly laid his hand on his lap, keeping it out of Maizie's reach.

She responded by removing her hand from the table top. Her face showed her disappointment in Gabriel's refusal to hold her hand.

He used his fork to point at his plate, "You're right, Maizie. This is really good poutine. The fresh curd makes it."

She didn't say anything. She sat quietly, chewing her wild rice. He knew he had offended her but what else was he to do? He made up his mind that if she made another pass at him, he would stop her from going any further. Letting her down easy so he didn't break her heart. He smiled at his own conceded thoughts. As though he was some Casanova, having to cast off an unwanted lover.

Seeing the smile on his face, Maizie's emotions switched to resentment. How could he be smiling after what he just did to her? 'Bastard!' she yelled in her head. She tossed her fork on her plate, the clatter of it echoing through the restaurant. Faces turned their way, curious as to what the commotion was.

Gabriel stopped chewing his steak and examined her face. She was definitely upset. Starting to chew again, he put down his fork and knife. "Maizie, is there something wrong? You don't look ... happy."

"Because I'm not." She sat up straight in her chair, looking him directly in the eye, her voice a loud whisper, "I thought this was a date. I thought you were interested in me." She leaned forward, her face tight with anger, "BUT YOU WON'T EVEN HOLD MY HAND. DAMN IT!" The last sentence was louder than she wanted it to be, again drawing stares from the other patrons.

He blew out a deep sigh. This was his chance to stop her advances. He carefully worded his explanation. "Maizie, I didn't mean this as a 'date-date' ... but as a lunch between friends." She was about to object, but he cut her off. "Maizie you're a beautiful woman but honestly, I'm still trying to get over my girlfriend's murder." He cursed

137

himself as soon as the words left his mouth — words he hadn't wanted to say to anyone.

Maizie pulled back in alarm. The question was asked cautiously, in a hushed voice, "Girlfriend's murder?"

He closed his eyes, wishing he could take back those last two words. But not being able to, he decided that it was best he told her the truth.

If there was anyone who needed to know the truth, it was Maizie.

ELEVEN

He tented his fingers in front of him, creating a barrier that would allow him to talk without looking directly into her face. He glanced her way, deciding if he should tell her part of it — or the whole story. If he did tell her the whole truth, he would be putting her in danger from Rene and Cash. But he could tell she genuinely cared about him — and it would be good to tell all the information to someone else before they came for him. "She was killed by two hit men from the Russian mob. They killed her because of what she knew." He swallowed down the lump building in his throat from the memory of his love, Heather.

"Heather was a freelance reporter for environmental issues here in Ontario and other regions of Canada. She was working on a piece about Aboriginal land being taken away from Reserves by large corporations that promised large numbers of jobs for the Indians that lived on those Reserves. But those jobs eventually went to white people."

Maizie nodded that she knew all too well what white man's greed could do to aboriginal communities. "Initially, they would hire the natives, paying them half of what the average white man got paid for doing the same work. If they complained, they found ways to let them go. Lack of skills or education. Or they would make up lies to fire them straight out. Like theft or drinking on the job." He sighed, "But that's not what got Heather murdered."

He then lowered his hands to look directly into her face, making sure she got every word of what he was about to tell her. Gabriel inhaled deeply to settle his nerves, before saying it out loud. Maizie would be the first person he told, making it even more difficult. He chose to be direct — only giving her the facts.

"She was shot in the head. Right in front of me. Outside our apartment." He swallowed down the next lump that formed in his throat. "I saw the two men who did it. And they saw me." He hung his head, "I've been running ever since."

She reached out and placed her hand over his, to comfort him, "Go on ..." she encouraged.

"While she worked on the Indian exploitation story, she would eat her lunch at the food court in the small mall down the street from where we lived. The energy of the space and its people, helped her with her writing. When she was blocked, she would 'people watch' while she sorted out her thoughts. What she began to notice was that several young women, girls really, would circle the mall over and over again. Then, when they reached the food court, a man would approach them, and they would leave together. Later the same girl would return to the food court and hand over an envelope to a guy sitting at one of the tables.

"At first, Heather didn't understand what was happening because she was only there for an hour or so at a time. But when it happened over and over again, with the same five or six teenaged girls, she finally put it together. The man at the table was their pimp and they were being approach by men inside the mall, going to a nearby motel for paid sex. That's when Heather began to keep detailed notes on the girls and how many tricks they did each day. She bought a separate notebook to record all the details. What the girls looked like. What they wore. The number of tricks they turned. Who the guys were or what they looked like. How long they were gone. If they had injuries or were upset. Everything went into that notebook. She even bought a small camera to take pictures of the girls and the bastard pimp." He took a deep drink of beer to wet his throat.

"But as a reporter, she couldn't just guess at what they were doing, she needed hard evidence. Heather followed one of the girls to the other side of the mall, out of the pimp's view. There she asked the teen if what Heather suspected, was in fact happening." His face pained, "You have to understand Maizie, these girls were no more than fourteen, fifteen years old. Young girls who should have been worrying about their first kiss or the latest hairstyles. Not having sex with disgusting old men in dirty motels. Heather said the girl was so scared, she folded in on herself, only nodding twice before running away from

141

her. That's when Heather had her proof." He exhaled a hard breath, so the heaviness in his chest didn't suffocate him. "I'm guessing the girl ran straight to her pimp and told him about her encounter with Heather. That was two days before they showed up in front of our apartment and shot her in the head." Tears filled his eyes. His body shook slightly from the sobs he tried to hold in.

Maizie squeezed his hand, wanting to hold him in his time of pain. "I'm so sorry ..." she patted his hand, not knowing what else to say while he silently wept.

After a few moments, he straightened his back, gathering himself together to continue the story. "I have her notebook. And they want it. Willing to kill me for it. I've been on the run ever since." He wiped his free hand over his face, removing the hot tears from his cheeks. "Where her camera went, I have no idea. Wish I had it. If I did, I could go straight to the cops with it. Or the newspapers." His jaw tightened, "Exposing those bastards would make her death worthwhile."

Walking up to the table, Twyla asked, "So, how's everything?" Her sunny voice seemed odd against the somber mood of their conversation.

Maizie snapped, "Oh for fuck sakes. Can't you just leave us alone?" She flipped her hair over her shoulder, "We'll call you if we need you." She waved her away with the back of her hand, "Now GET."

Twyla stuck her nose in the air and turned away with a 'Humph'

He scolded her, "That wasn't nice. She was just doing her job, Maizie."

"I was just stopping her from seeing you … upset."

"Still doesn't give you the right to be that rude." With the focus taken away from Heather's murder, he picked up his utensils and attempted to go back to eating his steak. Underneath the table, the side of his right foot tapped his left ankle, his mind focused on and counting each time they touched.

Maizie, still stunned by the account of Heather's death, only picked at her vegetables. She chewed on a mouthful of carrot while she watched calmness wash over Gabriel. How could he be so composed after telling her such a devastating story? Had his pain been so deep, so intense, that he could turn himself hard to his emotions. Question after question filled her thoughts. But there was one she wanted the answer to. "How long have you been on the run?"

His shoulders slumped as he said it, "Four months." The words expressed his exhaustion of always being on the run.

"Wow, that's a long time." Maizie was slowly putting the pieces together in her mind. "Is that why your car is parked behind the motel?"

Through a mouthful of steak, the words slightly muffled, "Partly. They have no idea what type of car I'm driving now. I kind of switched it out for another one." He anticipated her next question, "And no, I didn't steal it."

She laughed at his comment. "Didn't think you did. You don't seem the type."

He smirked, "I'm now the owner of an old beat up, 1980 Cavalier. And the fact that the hood doesn't quite match the rest of the body helps. I'm sure they'll be looking for an upscale, newer vehicle like the one I had driven before. I was lucky to stumble across the old heap on the roadside. I saw the faded FOR SALE sign tucked in the windshield. I parked my car in the nearby Canadian Tire parking lot, removed those plates, grabbed my backpack, and walked to where the car was sitting in the old woman's yard.

"After a fair bit of haggling ... mostly to look like I was normal and not on the run ... we came to a price we both could agree on. Five-hundred-dollars. CASH ... I insisted. Truth was, I would have paid four times that price just to have a car they wouldn't be looking for. I knew it would only be temporary but one day ahead of the men hunting me was a blessing. The greater the distance between me and them, the better for me. I drove off, my backpack safely on the passenger's seat. Two towns over, I exchanged my plates for those of another Cavalier, same years and same make of car. More to confuse the local cops than anything else. So far, I have been lucky that no one has bothered with the middle-aged guy in the baseball cap, driving an old heap, minding his own business.

"My worn clothes and black baseball cap are also part of my disguise. I traded in my button-down white shirt and tie for comfy blue jeans and t-shirts. But my biggest concealment was letting my beard grow rough and long, instead of being clean shaven. I even took on a heavy limp to throw off my gait, presenting myself as someone disabled. No one bothers with the disabled. They ignore them like they were some kind of nuisance. That allowed me to buy gas and take-out meals without worry of being remembered."

She swallowed down her mouthful, "So that's the reason you look so scruffy." It was finally all making sense to her. Pieces fitting into pieces, the puzzle showing itself. And his disheveled look was his way of camouflaging his appearance.

With unburdening his heavyweight, he found he was ready to be his humorous self again. "Scruffy?" He covered his heart with his hand, "I'm wounded."

She laughed at his joke but took the opportunity handed her. "Well, somewhere under all that scruff, I see a handsome man." Her face flushed with her admission that she had looked intimately enough to see the man behind the beard and unkempt hair. Yet she fluttered her lashes in his direction, telling him she was still interested in him. "And honestly ... no man would be caught dead looking so raggedy."

Twyla had made her way to a spot behind Maizie and was signaling Gabriel with her hands, asking if they needed more drinks. He waved her over, "It's okay. Maizie promises to behave herself."

"Speak for yourself," Maizie muttered back.

Twyla only faced Gabriel, her back turned to Maizie, "Did you need anything else to drink?"

Gabriel shook his head. Maizie piped up, "I'll have another red wine."

Gabriel added the 'please' for her.

Maizie refused to say it.

Twyla glanced in her direction, the one lazy eye appearing to scoff at Maizie. The waitress left with her head held even higher, triumphant that she had won that round.

He had no idea why Maizie was being so malicious towards the waitress but he also didn't feel like playing referee between the two women. He continued to eat his steak in silence. Twyla returned, placing the wine glass closer to Gabriel, making it just out of Maizie's reach. She spoke to Gabriel only, "There you go. Do you need anything else? Dessert perhaps?"

Having enough of their catlike sparring, he almost yelled, "No!" He smiled so as to not offend her, "No, we're fine. Just the bill, thank you."

Once Twyla was out of earshot, Maizie complained, "She ruined our lunch."

Gabriel said it harshly, "No ... YOU ruined our lunch. She was doing her job." He cut the last piece of his steak in two and stuffed one half in his mouth. He avoided her eyes, but said it clearly so she heard him, "Jealousy is never becoming."

She closed her mouth with a snap. It was true. She had been jealous and he had seen it. She concentrated on the last of her trout, pushing it about her plate. When Twyla came with the bill, Maizie focused on her plate, trying her hardest to keep her comments for Twyla to herself.

Through the last piece of steak, he complimented Maizie. "You were right. This has been one of the best meals I've had in a long time. Thank you for recommending this place."

It brought a smile back to her face. "And thank you for the company." She knew inside she had made a major mistake fighting with Twyla. Her mind raced as to how she was going to repair the damage she had done. She reached for the bill.

But Gabriel grabbed it a second before she did. "Nope. My treat."

She sat up straight, "Then I insist on leaving the tip." That, she realized, would be how she would make it up to Twyla. She reached in her clutch and pulled out a twenty-dollar bill. She tucked it under her plate so only the edge was sticking out. "That should do it," she said quietly, glancing at his eyes for approval. He gave her none.

Gabriel left two twenties on top of the bill. "Shall we go? I think I need to walk this off ... or maybe a giant nap."

Maizie laughed, "If you napped, your stomach would never forgive you. A walk would be better." In actuality, she was encouraging the walk because she wanted to spend more time with him. "We could go down to the river again. See if any bears show up."

His stomach growled loudly, "I think I'm going to head back to the motel. I'm feeling rather sleepy now." He wasn't actually tired, he was doing his best to evade her. The less time he spent with her, the less likely she was to get her hopes up.

She was disappointed but was hopeful that she could convince him to a nap in her bed instead. "Great. Let's go."

As they exited the restaurant door, Twyla called after them, "Thank you! Please come again!" While waiting for Maizie to do up her coat against the chilling winds, Gabriel witness through the front window Twyla's surprise when she removed the dirty plates. Her mouth hung open at the shock of finding Maizie's twenty-dollar tip. Another smile of victory washed across her face and she stepped lively out of site.

"Okay, all set." She looked for his hand to hold, but he had them stuck inside his pockets. Gabriel walked ahead of her, keeping a steady pace, not giving Maizie the opportunity to touch him in any way. After two blocks, Maizie was out of breath, "Oh my lord. Slow down, long legs."

Gabriel laughed, "Sorry. I'm used to walking with Heather. She was as tall as me and her legs were even longer."

She picked up on the sadness in his voice. "You miss her, don't you?"

"More than life itself." A statement that was truer than Maizie could ever comprehend.

They continued to walk in silence, Maizie unsure what to say to a man who had watched his girlfriend die.

Gabriel's silence was because he was trying his hardest not to cry. His sorrow weighed heavy on his chest, making it hard for him to breathe. They rounded the corner onto Main Street and waited for an old clunker truck to go by. Just as it cleared the intersection, a pipe on its rack slipped, falling against the bed of the truck.

The sharp bang sounded identical to the gun that shot Heather dead. Gabriel reacted to it, his body going into overdrive with terror. He immediately cowered to the sidewalk, crouching as low as he could for protection.

In his mind, images of Heather's murder flashed.

Gunshot.

Bits of brain on his arm and face.

Heather falling to the ground.

Blood pooling on the cement.

The sound of squealing tires.

Panic.

On the sidewalk beside Maizie, he broke out into a sweat, his heart hammered in his chest.

Maizie wasn't sure what was happening to him, "Gabriel, what is it?"

He reached up and pulled her down to the ground with him. "Get down." He scanned the streets around them, looking for any signs of Rene and Cash.

"What are you looking for?" His behavior was scaring her.

He pulled her along with him, crawling to the side of the nearest building. With his back against the wall, and feeling somewhat safe, he finally answered her. "Them. I'm looking for them."

"Who?"

"The men chasing me."

"It was the truck. A pipe fell." She put her hand on his knee. "Gabriel, there's no one there. It was only the truck."

He was trembling, his muscles taut with fear, "Are you sure? They could be hiding."

Maizie stood up and walked away from the wall he had pulled her to. "There's no one there. Look!" she swung her arms to prove her point. "No one." She bent over him,

"Gabriel, you're safe. We are safe." She held out her hand for him to grab. "Come on, let's go."

Reluctantly, he took her hand and pulled himself up. Not trusting her instincts, he stopped at the edge of the building and peeked around it, looking in all directions for the men who had been hunting him. They weren't there. Not in the doorways or alley entrances. Maizie was right, it was just the truck. It must have been the combination of the pipe falling and his intense feeling of sorrow for Heather that triggered his reaction. He took his first steps past the building's edge, meeting Maizie at the intersection itself.

"Are you okay? Jesus, you scared me."

He just nodded rapidly. He swallowed several times to loosen the tightness in his throat. "I'm good now." His hand dropped to his side, his first two fingers tapping against his outer leg. He concentrated on the taps, feeling the impact against his fingertips. The image of the old man who taught him the self-relaxing technique lingered in his mind.

She took his elbow, "Let's get you back to your room. You're white as a ghost."

He repeated himself, "Sorry."

"Don't be sorry. You've been traumatized. It makes perfect sense that you'd react this way." Her voice was soft and soothing, "We'll get back to the motel and we can relax in bed. Would you like that?"

He couldn't believe she was still pushing him to be with her. "By myself ... yes."

Her heart sank that he didn't fall for her ploy. "Uh, yah ... that's what I meant."

He knew better but didn't have the strength to deal with it right then. They walked on down the main street, passing Stedmans and Kathi's Kitchen. Approaching the hardware store, it reminded him that he was still had to get the ten-foot piece of rope for tomorrow night. More than ever he wanted to end his life. To end the suffering he was currently experiencing. He wanted to stop the hurt from Heather's death. He wanted to stop being terrified. He just wanted OUT. He crumbled again, folding down upon himself.

Maizie grabbed him around the waist, "Hang on. Only a few more blocks to go." She held him up, allowing him to move forward with less effort. "You can do this. You've come this far, you can surely make it another few blocks." She felt his body relax a little with her last statement. She talked as they walked along, hoping it would distract his mind from his overwhelming trauma. "And here's the barber shop you should visit. They'll take care of that scruffy hair. Red will give you a proper haircut and a good shave. He's a master with a straight blade." She felt him slide again. With a grunt she pulled his hip against her ribs, steadying his body. Come on Gabriel, work with me here. I'm too short to carry you."

"Sorry." He stopped walking, "Give me a second." He inhaled through his nose and braced his knees. He told himself to fight it, to get a grip on himself. He continued to tap on himself, relieving the panic inside him. "Okay, here I go." She held on to him while he stood on his own, his back rigid and his knees locked. He gently pushed back her arm, "I'm good. But can we go right back to the motel? I'm not sure how much longer I can do this." He honestly felt like curling up right there on the cement, giving up his struggle altogether. But it was the old man's words that pushed him forward. He had warned Gabriel — 'Don't give in to it. If you do, you'll never get out of it.'

Together they walked back to the motel, Gabriel walking slowly, and Maizie holding out her arm, ready to catch him if he collapsed again. By the time the motel was in view, he was standing tall, his trauma nearly subsided. "Almost there." She encouraged, "One more block. Just got to get to the motel and across the parking lot."

"Good," was all he said. By the time they reached the motel, Gabriel had forced himself to be normal, walking as though nothing was wrong. He didn't need to tap any longer.

As they passed the office's front window, she spoke up, "You're looking better. Your colors back." She held her breath before she asked, "Do you want to come back to my room ... or should we go to your room?"

"Maizie ..."

He didn't need to finish the sentence, she knew the answer. "That's fine. I'll walk you to your door."

"Like hell, you will." He aimed her towards the sidewalk running down her side of the motel courtyard. "I'm going to walk you to YOUR door." Seeing the glimmer of hope in her eyes, he quickly added, "Then I'm going to my room alone to rest." He saw her shoulders fall slightly with disappointment.

Before them, sitting outside his room, was the man that belonged to the blue pickup truck. He was smoking a cigar and the beer bottle in his hand was half-empty. For some unknown reason, Gabriel's gut instinct told him to lower his head and turn it away from the stranger.

Maizie greeted him with a professional tone, "Good afternoon, Mr. Dallas. Are you enjoying your stay?"

He nodded that he was. In truth, he was ignoring her, while attempting to get a look at the man walking with her. But from where he sat, he couldn't get a clear look at his face. He relaxed, thinking the man he was looking for was no scruffy bum. He was an upper-class preppy bastard. Well groomed with tailored clothes. Not a plaid-wearing guy straight out of the bush.

"Do you need anything, sir? More towels, perhaps?"

"No thank you. I am good for now." He stretched himself tall, trying to get a glimpse of the man's face. Unfortunately, by then, they had walked passed his sight line.

Gabriel noted the slight accent in the man's voice — Russian.

"Well, you enjoy your evening then," Maizie said over her shoulder.

Dallas watched after them, as they made their way to Maizie's door.

Gabriel glanced over his shoulder into the reflection of the window across the courtyard. As he feared the man was intently staring at him. The hair on Gabriel's neck stood on end. He might not have been Rene or Cash, but there was a sense of threat from the man watching him. As he had done many times before, Gabriel added a limp to his walk. No one was looking for a man that limped.

Reaching her doorway, Gabriel bent down and hugged her, a motion she happily accepted. Still hugging her, his face turned away from Dallas, he whispered in her ear, "Maizie, that man, how long has he been here?"

She, in turn, whispered back, "He arrived two days after you did. Why?"

"Don't react to what I'm about to say. We must act normal." He felt her head nod against his shoulder. "I think he's here to find me." Her being silent, he didn't think she understood. "He's here to kill me, Maizie."

Her body tensed, "Oh, shit." She went to pull away from Gabriel but he held her in place.

"Shhh. Stay calm." He pulled away from her, keeping her in place with a hand on each shoulder. "I'm not a hundred percent sure so until he does something, I'll consider him just another stranger in town." His head furrowed, "I'm going to return to my room now. I still have so much work to do before tomorrow night."

"Tomorrow night? What's happening tomorrow night?"

"Don't worry about that. Now go into your room like you know nothing. Act normal." He hugged her one more time and let her go. He turned and limped back to his room using the sidewalk running along the back rooms of the courtyard.

Dallas watched Gabriel as he went, trying to catch a glimpse of his entire face. But the man disappeared into his room without Dallas getting a thorough look. He butted out his cigar and went directly inside his room, his guts telling him to watch the man's door, to see him when he comes out again. He placed the chair in front of his window and parted the sheers slightly — just enough to get a clear view of the door to room 13.

~

Gord's teeth hurt from grinding his anger at the sight of Gabriel hugging his Maizie. "You son of a bitch," he muttered under his breath. He was tempted to trash his office again but decided he didn't feel like cleaning it up one more time. He settled for punching his legs again. "That's it city boy. After tomorrow night, you're out of here." He jabbed his finger in Gabriel's direction as he limped back to room 13, "She's my girl ... you bastard. Not yours."

The other thing that caught his eye was the Russian's movements. Dallas was watching Gabriel closely, stretching his neck to see where he was going. Was there a connection between Gabriel and the Russian? And if so, were the people in his motel in danger? His gut told him to do the one thing he made a point of never doing. He went into his private room and took down his Winchester .308 semi-automatic rifle. He loaded it with bullets and went back out in the office where he leaned it against the filing cabinet closest to the window. He draped the curtain over it so only the bottom of the butt showed below its hem. If the Russian was connected to Gabriel, Gord was going to protect his people — even if that meant shooting both the

Russian AND Gabriel. The idea of shooting the latter made him smile with wicked intent.

~

Inside his room, Gabriel panicked.

He paced back and forth, unsure of what to do next. Should he just grab his backpack and run? Or stay put, completing his mission of telling the world what Heather had discovered.

What Heather had died for.

The thick belt sitting on the dresser top answered his question. He would stay. He would do the work he needed to do to save the girls in Heather's black notebook. Then he would end his life, stopping the pain in his heart.

TWELVE

Gabriel had worked until 4 AM, carefully transcribing Heather's notes into a detailed chart system that could easily be understood — and photocopied. He hand-wrote each letter, pleading with the recipient to either investigate her findings or publish them in their newspaper. He had addressed the envelopes to save time when he returned from town with the photocopies. Only when every last detail had been completed and he had stuffed everything under the padded cover of the box spring, did he finally attempt to fall asleep. He felt confident that if he was killed in his sleep or during his trip to town, Maizie would eventually find them. He hoped she would know what to do next and mail them all with no one stopping her. Lying in bed, he thought about Heather.

How they met and their time together.

The way she encouraged his writing, telling him he was getting better with each page he wrote. She, of course, was lying and he knew it. But her loving, supportive words still made him feel as though he could go on writing — not giving up completely. It was also the way she laughed. Her backward giggle that initially drew his attention the first night they met ...

He was sitting at a table in the corner of the bar, his friends bitching about work and their significant others, when he heard a peculiar laugh come from the other side of the jam-packed bar. When he heard it the second time, he knew he had to see who the person was that laughed in such a bizarre manner. Character information for a novel he had not written yet, he told himself. When his eyes found the woman the laugh came from, he fell in love instantly.

She was laughing freely at someone's joke, her head tilted back with abandon, exposing her long lean neck. A neck he desperately wanted to kiss. But what really attracted him was that she appeared as free as her laugh. Her hair was long and loose, her clothing Bohemian in style. Next to no makeup, allowing her own beauty to shine. Luck was on his side, the woman sitting beside her knew him, calling Gabriel over to join them. And he did, making sure he was sitting next to the woman he knew in his soul he had to meet. As the evening wore on and people began to depart, it left only him and the red-headed goddess he wanted to know better. When last call was announced, she batted her eyes at him, suggesting they take their conversation back to her place. Gabriel remembered that his heart erupted with both excitement and fear. He was ecstatic that he was going to her place, presenting the possibility of forming a relationship with her. Or at least, if the stars aligned, they would share a night of crazed sex.

The latter happened without hesitation. Neither one holding back their emotions or passion, giving themselves freely to the other. When morning came, their heads on the pillows, he asked if he could stay with her forever. At first, she laughed her backward giggle, brushing off his silliness as sexual enthusiasm. But when he called that night, she told him to bring his toothbrush and a few changes of clothing for a trial run. In a whirlwind romance, he left behind his crappy apartment and began his life with her — loving, supportive, and always Bohemian. Having the life of a freelance reporter, her hours were flexible, random rather than scheduled.

He fell asleep, his heart filled with both love and anguish for the memory of his Heather. The morning would bring him to his final day in pain. By nightfall he would be dead, killed by his own doing.

~

From the chair at his desk, Gord watched Gabriel slip out his door, lock it, his face down and turned away from the Russian's room. He limped past the office, his hands tucked in his pockets. Why was he suddenly limping? Had he limped before and Gord not notice? Gord even made a point of going outside to watch him walk down the street. When Gabriel disappeared into a building, Gord headed back inside, the chilly wind giving him goosebumps. At least he assumed it was the wind.

Back at his desk, he watched Maizie make her rounds as she always had. But this time, he noticed she was constantly looking towards room 2 — the Russian's room. Did she know something that he didn't about the man with the blue truck? There were so many questions running through Gord's mind, he was getting a headache again. It was either stress or the lack of sleep from keeping vigil all night long. Watching for any trouble Gabriel might have brought their way. He rubbed his tired eyes with the backs of his hands, grumbling under his breath, "One more day, city boy ... then you're outta here."

~

On the way to town, Maizie's words echoed in his head. 'No man would be caught dead looking so raggedy.' She was right. Even though it was him that was going to end his own life, he should at least be a presentable corpse. He would stop at the barber shop Maizie mentioned. A proper haircut and an old-fashioned shave were definitely in order. But only after he photocopied the chart. Since he had no idea where to find a photocopier in the small town, he stopped at Stedmans for directions.

"We only have three in town. One is at the lawyer's office. Townhall ... but it's closed today. And the other is in my back room." She smiled shrewdly, "And I only charge ten cents a copy."

His phony smile equaled her's, "That's not a problem. Show me the way."

"Don't mind the mess. It's a storage area so we don't bother too much with dusting and such." She pulled back the black curtain allowing him to duck under it ahead of her. She pointed, "It's over there." Just then the front door chimed that a customer came in. "You just come see me when you're done and we'll figure out what you owe." The little bell on the front desk 'dinged' that her customer was impatient. "HOLD YOUR COTTON PICKING HORSES!" she yelled before reaching the curtain again. She smiled back to Gabriel and pointed with her finger, "Power button is on the side. The green one." The bell dinged again, making her even madder. "TOUCH THAT BELL ONE MORE TIME AND YOU'LL NEVER USE THAT HAND AGAIN." She pushed the curtain aside and disappeared around it, "Damn you, Jean. What's your flippin' hurry?"

Glad she was gone, Gabriel turned on the machine and lined up his copy of the chart along the side. Once it was warmed up, he copied off one to see what it looked like. Too dark. He adjusted it, by pushing the minus button, and printed off another. Perfect. He punched in twenty-six and watched as the copier printed off twenty-six identical copies of his chart. He heard the door chimes beyond the curtain seconds before the copier stopped. He flipped through them, making sure each one was printed properly. He removed his original and stacked all the copies together. Under the curtain he went and made his way to the front desk. There the clerk was dealing with a pile of photo envelope sorting. Checking each one off her master list with hard pencil marks like she was angry with whoever just left. As he approached, she inhaled through her nose and replaced her irritated, lip-pinching frown with a fake grin. "All done then? How many did you copy?"

"Twenty-eight."

Her words were curt, "Anything else?"

"Stamps."

"They come in sheets of ten. How many you want?"

He held up three fingers.

She started to ring it all in but he handed her a twenty-dollar bill, "That should cover it. And a bit extra for being so helpful."

"Well, that's mighty nice of you." Her face lit up, lifting off her scowl. "Let me put all that in a bag for you. To keep them clean." She pulled a red bag off the peg and grabbed for his papers.

"No!" Not wanting her to read what was on the pages, he insisted, "I'll do it myself, thanks." He took the bag from her and slipped the copies inside, adding the stamps last. "Thanks again." He left her there behind the counter, her mouth open, and the twenty taut between her fingers, looking as though she didn't believe the money to be real.

He retraced his steps, heading for Red's Barber Shop. Stepping through the door, it wasn't hard to figure out which one was Red. He had a full head of ginger hair and a pair of scissors in his hand. He nodded Gabriel's way and returned to his snipping. Seeing that Red was already trimming someone's hair, Gabriel took a seat on the bench beside the other three men that were talking amongst themselves.

The last man on the bench continued where he left off, "So she says, well if you like your pot roast moist like my mother's, you should'a married my mother." All the men laughed at his joke. "Then she took my plate away and

162

threw it in the trash … plate and all." That brought on another round of chuckles.

"You never learn do you, Harold?"

"Guess not." He snickered, "But then again, she ain't learn to cook like her mother neither!" More laughter.

Red held up the hand mirror to show the man in the chair the back of his head. A firm nod signaled Red got it right. He loosened the plastic cape off the customer and let him out of the chair. The happy customer laid a ten on the shelf under the mirror and wished everyone a good day, not joining the older men on the bench.

Red looked at Gabriel and softly patted the back of the chair. "You're up son."

"Um … they were here first."

Red snorted, "They aren't here to get their hair cut. They're here to bitch about their wives and gossip." Laughter erupted from the men. Heads nodded that Red was telling the truth. It was a place they could meet that their wives didn't dare poke their noses into.

Gabriel slipped into the seat and Red put a fresh cape around his neck. "So, what are you looking for today, son."

"Christ by the looks of him … a lot of everything!" taunted Harold.

Even Gabriel laughed at his joke. He also caught a glimpse of Red shooting Harold a dirty look, silently telling him to shut up. To ease the situation, Gabriel agreed, "Man's right. A haircut and a straight shave."

Red nodded. "What are we looking at here? Short on the sides, long on the top?"

Gabriel pointed to the man in the middle of the bench, "Like his."

"Oh, a Dale Special," joked Harold with finger quotes.

"Shut up," snapped Dale.

"Oh, come on. You know I'm just funnin' ya."

Not wanting to go at it with Harold, Dale adjusted himself on the bench and re-crossed his legs. "I just like to be presentable, is all."

In the mirror, Gabriel watched Red give Harold another 'behave' look and that made Harold blow out a huff of disapproval. Gabriel quickly understood that these men were longtime friends that knew each other all too well.

Red sprayed down Gabriel's hair and started combing out all the long scraggly ends. "You been in the bush or something? Ain't seen hair this outta shape on purpose."

"Been traveling," was all Gabriel said. He was trying to stay private without drawing attention to himself.

"That'll do it." Red pulled his scissors from his breast pocket and dipped it in the blue jar on the shelf. He wiped it on the towel hanging below it and started his first cuts. Off came the long ends, immediately improving Gabriel's appearance. As he thinned down the sides and worked on the shape of his hair, Harold started another story of his home life.

"The wife's sister was over two nights ago. Hot damn boys, if she wasn't wearing one of those mini skirts of hers. Reached up for a dish on the top shelf of the cupboard and whoooo-wee, I got me an eye full of Becky's bare ass."

That caught Dale's attention. "That be a fine ass too."

The other man chortled, "And you otta know!"

Dale's face lit up as he bragged about his conquest, "Damn straight I do, Phil."

Harold roared, "Yah, you and every other guy with a dick in this town."

"Shut up," snapped Dale.

"Damn, you're sensitive today. You on your period or somethin'?"

Red snorted at that shot.

In the mirror, Gabriel was starting to look more like his old self. Trim and professional.

"Gonna lower you, so hold on." Red lowered the back of the chair so that Gabriel was leaning flat out backward. From the chrome box in the corner, Red brought out a towel with tongs, its steam drifting off the top. He carefully draped the hot cloth over Gabriel's face, making sure he covered every inch of his skin. "Now we have to let that do its work for about five minutes. You relax while I get my shavin' gear ready."

From under the towel, Gabriel heard the shop's door open and close. Harold welcomed the newcomer, "Hey ya, Luke. What's new in your part of the woods?"

He slid in beside Phil, "Guess you haven't heard then."

"Why? What'd we miss?" Dale peaked around Phil.

Luke hung his head as he spoke, "There's been a death at the Parker place."

Phil, a long-time friend of the Parker's, spoke up, "Oh damn. Who?"

"Young Jocelyn."

Gasps filled the air.

"She done hung herself."

Phil's head whipped Luke's way, "What?!"

Hearing the words 'hung herself,' Gabriel's head turn his way too. Red grabbed hold of the towel before it fell off. "Hold on there, young man. Don't be turning like that. You'll lose the heat of the towel." Gabriel turned straight ahead again but listened intently to the men's conversation.

"When she didn't come down for breakfast or lunch, they checked her room but she wasn't there. They went looking for her. Everyone fanned out across the property, searching the yard, fields, and buildings." He stopped for a moment to swallow down the lump in his throat, "Her Ma found her hanging from the rafters. She screamed and screamed until the rest of them found her hysterical on the floor. Their boys had to forcibly pull her out of the barn. They say she's so distraught she can't talk. Just stares at nothing."

"Holy Jesus," someone muttered, half a curse, half a prayer.

The men were quiet for a moment, each in their own thoughts about what had happened to both the young girl and the people they considered to be good friends and neighbors.

So was Gabriel.

For the first time, he had thought about who was going to find him tomorrow when he completed his plans of suicide. It would be Maizie who found him hanging from the bathroom door. And then Gord. His stomach churned at the realization that the flirty housekeeper would be as

166

traumatized as the mother who found her daughter. Just then, Red uncurled the towel from his head, exposing his distraught face to everyone else in the room. He quickly covered up his expression of concern for Maizie by hissing out, "Damn, that's hot." He tilted his head towards the men on the bench. Harold was quiet and Phil wiping away tears with the back of his wrist.

Luke continued, the words so soft, Gabriel could barely hear them. "They found her diary. She wrote that she was raped at college by two football jocks that got her drunk. Maybe slipped her drugs. Who knows. She passed out and they did whatever they wanted. Then the bastards bragged to everyone what they did to her. When she reported it to the police ... they did nothing. She said they told her because she was drinking with them, she wanted it, and was 'crying wolf' to save her reputation."

"Bastards!" swore Phil.

Red showed Gabriel the blade, "You ready?" When he nodded he was, Red said, "Good. Now don't do that again until I'm done. I don't like the sight of blood." Gabriel smiled at his joke but inside he was not only experiencing the sorrow of the men sitting on the bench, he was also dealing with the heavy revelation that someone else would be affected by the act of taking his own life. Through his churning emotions, he barely felt the thick lather being swirled over his face in preparation for the blade.

"Damn shame," Harold's voice was on the verge of cracking. "She's the same age as my granddaughter."

The metal blade slid across his cheek, gently tugging at the hairs of his scruffy beard, leaving behind the feel of cool air against his stripped skin. To stop the turmoil in his mind, he concentrated on the sensation of the blade against his face. Stroke by stroke, the unkempt Gabriel disappeared, replaced by the former man he was. Red used the steam towel to wipe away the last bits of shaving cream from Gabriel's face. "There you go, young man. You look civilized again." He stepped on the back of the chair and lifted Gabriel to an upright position.

Gabriel could only stare at himself. In the mirror before him, was the reflection of the man he once was — clean cut Gabriel Carr.

That man also acknowledged one more truth.

He no longer wanted to kill himself as he had planned.

That man was determined to spare Maizie the horrors of finding him dead.

"Well damn. You clean up good, son. I would not recognize you as the man who walked in here thirty minutes ago." Red knew he had to break the somber mood from the bench. "Don't you think so boys?"

Dale looked up and examined Gabriel's face. "Hell, you're right Red. Looks like a completely different guy."

Phil, wanting to lift his own spirits, teased him too. "Son, if I wasn't a man, I'd ask you out on a date."

"Maybe my sister-in-law Becky can ask him!" barked Harold, bring on an outburst of laughs.

Red held up the mirror, showing the neat trim line of the back. Gabriel, being overwhelmed, only nodded for fear he would start weeping if he spoke. He placed two twenties on the shelf, nodded his thanks to Red, and quickly rushed out the door.

Harold looked past the other men on the bench at the closing door. "Well, wasn't he a talkative little shit?" Dale laughed first, followed by the rest of them.

~

Outside the chilling winds slapped Gabriel in his newly naked face. No longer was it protected by the shaggy, rough beard. The same wind blew over his exposed ears settling down in his collar. He shivered as he walked, his mind racing with the new decisions he had to make. No longer wanting to kill himself where Maizie would find him, he had to figure out his next moves.

The first was obvious. He had to finish stuffing the envelopes with the photocopies and letters, then mail them as soon as possible. After that was accomplished, he was free to do what he wanted — what he needed to do. Another gust of cold stung his cheeks, making him pull his collar up as high as he could. He hunched down into its red plaid warmth for protection against the wind that was funneling down the small main street.

By the time he reached the edge of the motel property, Gabriel had formulated a plan that not only saved Maizie from the horrors of finding him hanging in his room, it also allowed him to leave quietly. With no fanfare or guilt.

The plan was to mail all the letters and return to the motel. He would do his best to sleep the afternoon away, gathering enough energy to complete the next step. In the middle of the night, he would get in his car and simply drive away — disappearing out of Maizie's life for good.

He would then drive east, filling up at the next gas station he found. Continuing north, he would drive down back roads until he ran out of gas. Wherever the car stopped, he would walk off into the bush and hang himself from a tree — finally ending his misery.

Still aware that the man named Dallas may be hunting him, he skirted along the front of the office and peeked around its corner. The truck was there, but the man wasn't outside. The curtains were also closed, making Gabriel believe he might be blocking out the light to sleep. Feeling it was safe, Gabriel stayed close to the walls of the office and headed straight to room 13, keeping his head facing away from Dallas's door. He limped down the sidewalk, his collar pulled high on his left-hand side. Reaching his door, he hurried to unlock it, shutting the door behind him without facing outside. Once the deadbolt was locked again, he hung his head and blew out a long-held breath.

Exhausted, he flopped on the bed, his coat still pulled up past his ears. He exhaled the tension he held in his chest and swallowed down the lump of fear in his throat. He unbuttoned his coat, letting the warm air of the room seep in. His simple trip to town had turned into a roller coaster of emotions. Unable to fight his feelings any further, he closed his eyes and let them all rush out at once. He wanted to cry yet couldn't. Overwhelmed, his mind had shut down, darkness invading his soul once more. He lay motionless, listening only to his breathing.

~

Dallas restlessly paced the length of his room, trying to decide what to do next. Should he go out on the road to search for Gabriel Carr as he had the past few days? Or stay at the motel to follow up on his hunch that the man staying in room 13 was indeed the man he had been hunting for all that time.

He opened a slit in the curtains just in time to see the door to room 13 close tight. He swore under his breath, "Son of a bitch." He had missed seeing the man's face again. A sinister smile slipped across his mouth. The fact was, he knew exactly where to find the man, if he wanted to. All he had to do was knock on his door, knowing the man would open it, exposing himself face to face. But not in broad daylight where people could become witnesses. He would have to wait until dark to pull off the plan without getting caught. He opened the curtains fully then flopped on the bed. He tucked his hands behind his head and laughed at his luck. All he had to do was stay on his bed and watch the door of room 13 from where he lay.

The reward money was as good as his.

Well, that is if it really was Gabriel Carr in room 13.

THIRTEEN

The red plastic bag slipped off the bed and dropped to the floor, pulling Gabriel out of his darkness. He lay on the bed, waiting until his mind cleared itself. He prepared himself for the next task of his day — the completion of Heather's letters to those Gabriel hoped would help the girls working the food court at the mall. His stomach growled, protesting its emptiness. But it would have to wait. His first priority was the letters.

He swung his feet off the bed and planted them on the ugly green carpet. He took off his coat and tossed it on the nearby chair. He knelt down and pushed the mattress off its box spring. From under the rip in the padded cover, he slid out the papers he had hid there the night before. Shoving the mattress back in place, he began sorting the letters and envelopes into individual piles, matching letters to addresses. He added a photocopy to each one, folding the stack in thirds before licking the envelopes gluey strip. He was halfway done when a knock came to his door.

She gently rapped her knuckles on the door and spoke through it, "It's Maizie." She waited patiently, but when he didn't come to the door, she knocked again.

Gabriel ignored her, continuing his stuffing and sealing of the envelopes.

She knocked a little louder, in case he was still sleeping. "It's Maizie," she said even louder.

He continued to ignore her, hoping she would take the hint and go away.

Pissed off that he wasn't answering, she hammered on the door with the heel of her fist, then yelled through it, "It's Maizie. Open the door."

"Go away ... I'm busy!" he yelled back.

She wasn't taking that for an answer. She hammered again, "It's me. Open up the door."

"God damn it. Go away!" He was so mad at her, his hands shook the papers he was trying to fold in thirds.

"No!" she hammered again. She yelled louder, "Gabriel! Open up, Gabriel!" her words reverberating through the courtyard.

Hearing his name being yelled outside, he raced to the door and flung it open. He grabbed her arm and yanked her inside, slamming it behind her.

~

Half-asleep Dallas sat up on top of his bed. Had he heard what he thought he heard? He raced to the window and looked through the sheers, just in time to see the maid disappear through the door of room 13. A hand wrapped around her arm pulling her inside. The maid's cart was left parked outside the room, looking both odd and abandoned.

He let the sheers go and paced the length of the room once more. Had he actually heard the name Gabriel screamed for everyone to hear? Or had he merely dreamt it? Could it have been his subconscious regurgitating information in his brain? No, he was sure he hadn't fully fallen asleep. At least, that's what he hoped had happened.

As he paced back from the bathroom, the one question occurred to him. How many guys named Gabriel could there be in that one shitty little town in the middle of Northern Ontario? Odds were only the one. The man in room 13 was the man he had been looking for all along. Gabriel Carr. The man Rene and Cash were desperate to find.

From his back pocket, he took out the photo he had of Gabriel and flipped it over for the scribbled phone number on the back. Believing he had found the man pictured in the photo, Dallas dove across the bed and reached for the motel's phone. If he was right, he would be a thousand dollars richer by the end of the day.

~

Leaning on the window frame of the rear office window, Gord had watched Maizie park her cart outside Gabriel's door. He saw her knock softly at first, then hammer on it like she was a crazy woman. Her lunatic behavior made him stand up straight, concerned for her safety when it came to the stranger inside that room. Then he heard her scream Gabriel's name at the closed door. "Shit!" Gord cursed, knowing damn well everyone else in the motel complex heard the name too. But what happened minutes later, worried him to the bone.

The light on the switchboard lit up that 'Dallas the Russian' was making an outside phone call. He didn't need to lift the receiver and listen in on the call. Gord's gut instincts knew trouble would be arriving at his motel in no time. He glanced at the butt of the Winchester sticking out from the curtain's hem.

He knew he had four rapid shots to take down whoever was coming.

After that, it was a losing battle.

~

"Ouch! That hurt!" She tried to yank her arm out of his grasp but he held on firm. She tugged again, "Stop it."

Beyond angry at what she had done, he shook her arm while he yelled at her. "What do you think you're doing yelling my name out loud? Telling everyone that I'm here … come kill me." He thrust her arm away, "Jesus, Maizie. Why don't you knock on Dallas's door and tell him I'm right here!" He was so furious she cowered against the wall, afraid he might hit her. "Are you trying to get me killed before I finish this?" his arm waved over the bed, showing her what he was working on.

That's when she first noticed all the envelopes and papers spread out on the covers. She stepped forward, her face curious, "Gabriel … what is all this?"

He snatched up a stack of papers and its corresponding envelope. "These are the letters to the newspapers, police stations, and a few lawyers." In angry determination, he shook the stack of papers in his hand above his head, "This is going to tell them all about the prostitution ring Heather found at the mall. About the mob pimps that are making money off little girl's bodies. Innocent children. The girl's in her notebook." He went silent, his anger replaced by sorrow. His hand fell to his side with sadness. Tears filled his eyes, "The reason Heather was murdered."

"Gabriel, I'm so sorry." She went to reach for him, to comfort him. Instead, he pushed her hand away. She lowered it, "Sorry I was only trying to help."

Seeing the hurt in her eyes, Gabriel sat down on the bed and dropped his head on his hands. "Sorry, Maizie. I'm just ..."

"... an asshole?" she finished, rubbing her arm where he had grabbed her. She sat down beside him, her other arm draped around his back. "Gabriel, it's okay. I know you're in pain. I know you have to do this." She rubbed up and down his back in a motherly motion while they sat silent for a few moments, his head still hung in grief. Softly, she offered, "Can I help?"

He raised his head and looked at her, gratitude in his eyes. "Yes. You can lick the envelopes. They're starting to taste gross."

That made her laugh. "Okay, where are we then?"

He stood, wiping the blurry tears from his eyes. He started by arranging the stacks that they had disturbed when sitting on the bed. "I'll stuff them and you lick." He handed her the stamps, "And add these too."

They worked side by side, quiet with concentration. Finally, Maizie spoke, "Tell me more about Heather's death."

At first, Gabriel hesitated. "Maizie, if I tell you, it can put you in danger."

She countered with logic, "But if you tell me, I can tell the police if anything should happen to you."

Since she knew much of the story already, he thought he might as well tell her the rest. He inhaled deeply to calm his nerves, then sat down on the edge of the bed and began.

"We were heading off to meet our friends for lunch like we did every other Sunday. I had forgotten my keys on the kitchen counter and went back upstairs to get them. Heather waited out front on the sidewalk for me to return. On the way back down, I heard a truck pull up beside our parked car. By the time I reached the bottom of the stairs, Heather was calling my name. From the doorway, I watched a man inside the truck shoot one bullet right into her forehead." He closed his eyes, recounting what he saw, "I can still see the bits of blood and flesh fly out the back of her head." He reopened his eyes, his shaky voice retelling his panic, "When another bullet hit the door frame beside my own head, I realized that he was shooting at me, wanting me dead as well. That's when I ran for it, down the side of our apartment building and jumped the fence at the third post. I knew from living there so long I would land directly in my neighbor's backyard. The neighbor with the two huge Rottweilers. They knew me so well from being neighbors, they didn't even think twice about me walking through their yard. Over my shoulder, I saw the heads of the guys in the truck pop up over the top of the fence, before they froze. They were met with growls and bared teeth, the dogs jumping as high as they could to bite at the strangers.

He laughed lightly, "I had no idea what happened with the dogs after that. I was too busy running for my life. I ran down back alleys and cut through parking lots, avoiding any roads the two men could easily drive down. I finally reached my destination, breathless and scared out of my mind. It was a place I hadn't been to in years. A place no one would think to look. I was under an old wooden boat, originally flipped upside down to keep the rain out. But that was years ago. Time had given it rotten patches and splits between the boards. All I knew is it was a safe place to hide from the two guys that wanted me dead."

"Dead," Maizie whispered, echoing his last word.

"I remembered the devastating feeling of knowing the love of my life was gone. Heather was dead. And I had watched it happen right in front of me." Tears welled up in his eyes, blurring the world. He held his breath trying not to sob in front of Maizie. But it was no use — he couldn't hold it back, he had to let it happen. Through trembling words, he continued, "She was dead. One minute we were going to a late lunch with friends and the next, she was dead, her body lying on the sidewalk." What had started as a soft whimper, turned into heart-wrenching sobs that eased the pain in his heart. Maizie stood next to him, her hand on his shoulder for comfort. Eventually, he stopped, his pain emptied again.

"Through the split between two boards, I could tell the sun was setting. It would be dark soon and I could leave my hiding spot. But go where? I couldn't go back to our apartment. For sure they'd be looking for me there. Go to the police? Or did the police think I was responsible for Heather's death? Had there been other witnesses to the shooting? It had been that time of the afternoon when the neighborhood was busy with people going shopping or coming back from mass." He inhaled deeply, before saying the next part. "Then I started to feel guilty. If I hadn't forgotten my damn keys, we would have been gone by then, missing the hit men altogether. Reality is, they would have found Heather no matter what. After that, I stopped my self-pity and got tough. I did what I needed to do to survive. I knew I had to go back, sneak into our apartment to pick up what I needed to go on the run. In my head, I made a list of things to grab and go. Cash, passport, clothing and most important, Heather's black notebook. Whoever those guys were, they killed Heather because she knew something they didn't want the law to know. And if that was the case, I knew they would be in her notes.

"Once it was completely dark, I made my way back to our apartment, retracing the route I used to get away. Three blocks from the apartment, I started looking at my surroundings. Was anything different? Was the truck they were driving still there? Were there strange cars not usually parked in the neighborhood? I listened. No dogs barking. That's always a good sign, you know. But by the time I climbed back over the Rottweiler's fence, I was sure someone was watching me. Heather had always told me,

'If you feel like you're being watched ... you are.' And trust me ... her reporter's gut was always right.

"I put my back to the rear wall of the apartment building and slid along it to the corner. I peeked around it, looking for any signs of the goons ... or the police. Although I couldn't see anyone, that feeling of being spied on was still bothering me. I slipped along the side wall, stopping at the front corner. A quick peek, revealed police tape and a cop car three spaces down the street. I took another look, this one longer, taking in more details. I couldn't believe my luck. The cop in the police car was sound asleep. No point in hesitating ... I went for it. I ducked under the police tape and crawled along the front shrubs until I reached our front door. Using the tiny pocket knife Heather had given me as a joke, I cut through the police tape X on the door and slipped inside. I closed the door tight behind me as quietly as I could. My gut told me to stop at the bottom of the steps and listen for sounds. In case the two men had come back. I heard nothing ... only eerie silence. I have to tell you Maizie, that void of sound, made every hair on my body prickle. Intuition told me something wasn't right. So I stayed motionless and listened longer. And that's when I heard it. The creak in the wooden floorboards of our living room. Someone was in our apartment waiting for me. Seconds later, I heard another creak, this one on the top landing. They were coming to get me. Not knowing what else to do, I slid along the side of the staircase, hiding in its shadow, my little pen knife ready to strike. Behind me, a door opened. It was the old lady who lived below us. Bella put her wrinkled finger to her lips, saying 'shhhh' without sound. She reached out and tugged on the back of my shirt, slowly pulling me inside. She closed the door quietly. Maizie, fear was etched on her old face, yet she bravely shoved me towards her back bedroom. Her keeping right on my heels. Once inside and the door locked, she finally spoke. No more than a faint whisper, but with that Jewish accent of hers, she scolded me like a little child. 'Gabriel, where have you been? The police have been trying to find you everywhere.' She even pointed her finger in my face like she was my mother."

He held up his hands, showing Maizie how he had protested, "I told her, I didn't do it. That it was two men that shot her. Jesus, these two guys show up in a pickup truck ... the one pulls out a handgun and shoots her. Right in front of me, I told her. She then tells me, 'We know dear.' She went to say more but stopped cold. She put her ear to the door, listening so hard she closed her eyes to hear better. She warned me with hand signals that whoever was upstairs, was now at the bottom of the steps. We both stayed still, not talking for fear he might hear us. That's when we heard a voice from the street. 'Police! Who's in there? Come out with your hands up where I can see them! I know you're in there.' We even heard the radio attached to the cop's hip. 'Back up is on its way. Out.'

"We both heard the sound of the man's footsteps change when he stepped on the mat outside Bella's door. Next, we heard the building's front door creak open. His attempt at the English language was badly mangled. 'Do not shoot. I am 'ere to visit my Auntie. I will go. I want no troubles.' But the cop wasn't buying it and shouted back,

'You crossed the police tape of a crime scene.' So he says, 'How else was I supposed to see my Auntie? She's so upset by horrible murder. I have come to ... to ... what is that word? Con ... con ... Constold?' The cop corrected him, 'Console. Look, visiting hour is over. You gotta go. Out of the building.' We heard the front door being closed and not much else for a bit. We heard the other cop car show up. 'He's gone,' yelled the first cop. We listened until there were no more voices. I was so relieved I remember crumbling against Bella's bedroom wall. That's when she hugged me and told me that Mrs. Foster across the street saw the whole thing. The police knew it wasn't me who murdered Heather. You have no idea how relieved I was to hear that." He blew out the same breath he was holding in his memory.

"But since I knew what Heather discovered involved organized crime, I still wasn't sure I could trust the police. Bella wanted to make me something to eat. I just wanted to get the hell out of there. Mostly I just wanted to protect Bella. So I left her apartment and went upstairs to ours. I grabbed my backpack and stuffed Heather's notebook inside. I was about to get my passport out of my dresser, when the closet door opened. It was the other guy ... and he had his gun aimed right at me."

Maizie gasped, "Jesus." She sat down beside him, eager to hear more.

"He shot at me but I rolled out of the way. I ran down the stairs and right into Bella. That old woman pushed me into her apartment with both hands then quietly closed and locked her door. She pointed to the open window in

182

her bedroom. It was at the back of the building. Meaning I didn't need to go out the front. I ran right to it and jumped out it. I climbed the fence again and headed back to the boat." He was quiet for a few moments, then added, "I have no idea what happened to Bella after that. I only hope she wasn't hurt by my attackers."

Maizie made the sign of the cross, her hands pressed together, sending a blessing for Bella's safety.

"I've never been back to find out." His shoulders slumped, "All I know is that Heather is dead." Tears filled his eyes, blurring Maizie's face. "… and I miss her."

Maizie was lost for words after hearing the truth about what happened to Gabriel's girlfriend. She only kept her arm around his waist while he sobbed.

His crying finally exhausted, he stood up, grabbed a sealed envelope by the end, and shook it at her, "So many people have been hurt by this Maizie, I have to get Heather's information to people who will do something with it."

She stood too, "Then let's get this finished. Then I can mail them for you."

"No!" The word was stern. "I must do it. I NEED to do it … if it's the last thing I ever do, I do this for Heather." Tears pooled in his eyes again. He wiped them away with the back of his wrist, determined not to start crying again. "It's my mission Maizie, not yours."

Her heart ached for Gabriel's pain. She handed him the next stack of papers and an envelope. "I understand."

He took them from her and put them down. "You need to go Maizie." He turned her around by her shoulders, "I can finish this by myself. And you need to stay safe." He opened the door, hiding himself behind it, "Time for me to finish what Heather started."

Maizie only nodded and left. Behind her the door closed and locked, the sound of the chain lock signifying she wasn't to return. That there was a great possibility that she would never see Gabriel again. Saddened by that reality, she pushed her cart back to the laundry room, stashed it away before returning to her own room. She too locked her door and slid the chain in place. They were little protection against the men Gabriel had described but it made her feel a bit safer.

~

Moses slowly made his way across the courtyard, enjoying the fresh cold air against his feverish skin. There was pain with each step he took. The cancer was progressing faster than the doctor had predicted it would. He wasn't sure if that was such a bad thing. The sooner he died, the sooner the pain would be gone. Once in his room, he would watch TV until he fell asleep. A routine he had recently adopted and thoroughly hated. And since he knew Tula liked to nap after her lunch of two deep whiskey's and a sandwich, he would keep the volume low, letting her sleep it off.

He carefully closed his door behind him, leaving the lock undone — just in case Tula wanted to visit like she did in the old days.

~

From the edge of his bed, Dallas watched Maizie return her cart to the laundry room. He was angry that he didn't get to see who was behind the door of room 13. One look at the man inside and he could have determined if it truly was Gabriel Carr, the man Rene and Cash wanted. He shrugged, "Guess I'll know in a few hours." Until then, he would bide his time by watching the door of room 13, making sure the man inside didn't leave. Moses came into view. He watched the old man make his way across the courtyard, each step a slow shuffle. Dallas wondered if he would ever make it to that age. In his business of being a hit man, a bullet generally ended your life long before old age ever would.

~

Tula had watched Moses make his way, each step filled with pain by the pinching of his face. Her heart went out to him. Oh, how she wanted to comfort him. To hold him like she used to. But those days were gone. Loudmouth Harold and suck-up Dale had teased Moses so much about their secret affair, he stopped coming around. And when he locked his door so she couldn't slip in unseen — she knew it was over. But the fact that he hadn't told her face to face, still hurt both her heart and her pride. A fact she took great pleasure in reminding him each time she hammered on his wall and yelled at him to turn down his TV. She often wondered if he played his TV too loud just to make her bang on the wall, connecting with her again. She heard him close his door — but no lock. She knew it was an invite, unfortunately, it was one she no longer wanted to accept.

~

Gord was relieved that Maizie was back in her room. The further away from Gabriel she was, the better. If who he thought was coming, he wanted her safely tucked inside her own room. He was looking forward to the city man being gone from their lives, whether it was by him being shot dead by the Russians or leaving on his own. Their lives could then go back to normal. Maizie taking care of his motel, and him taking care of her.

Moses came into view, his old body slower than the previous week. But that was to be expected from a senior with colon cancer. Gord had found out months ago by mistake. At the coffee shop, his nurse asked Gord how Moses had done after his last chemo. Much vomiting? Eating well again? Finding out Gord knew nothing about the elder's condition, she was mortified that she had leaked the senior's secret about his cancer. Red-faced, she made him promise not to tell anyone she had broken Moses's confidence. Also knowing she could lose her job over the indiscretion, Gord agreed he would keep the private information to himself.

He looked at the clock again, wondering how long it had been since Dallas had made his one phone call. He had been tempted to listen in on the Russian's call. But he also knew if he was heard listening, he would be killed as well, leaving no witnesses behind.

He sat down at his desk, looking over the quiet courtyard.

But how much longer it stayed quiet was anyone's guess.

FOURTEEN

For the last two hours, Gord had done sentry duty over the courtyard. Yet nothing had happened in that time. Everyone had stayed in their rooms, not even opening their curtains to look out their windows. Gord should have felt relieved but somehow, he wasn't. An ominous tension hung in the air, making his senses sharper than they normally would be. He stopped himself from pouring another cup of coffee, thinking that the six he already had was three too many. He walked back to his desk and tried to relax in his chair but his leg insisted on jiggling in place. Through the front window, he watched a black Cadillac stop at the motel's driveway, waiting for a van to go by. Once through, the luxury car turned in, bypassing the front office.

Gord wondered who the hell they thought they were, pulling into HIS courtyard like they owned the damn place. When they parked in front of Dallas's room, he immediately understood who they were visiting. The

Russian. And when the two men exited the caddy, he knew exactly who they were.

The descriptions Gabriel had given Gord fit the two perfectly. Tall, blonde ponytail with a white mustache. And the other was shorter, slim, and balding. "Shit, hell, damn." Rene and Cash were here at his motel. Two murderers looking for the man hiding in room 13.

He quickly picked up the phone on his desk to dial Gabriel's room, to warn him. Then he hesitated, the receiver hanging limply in his hand. In his mind, he realized that if he didn't warn Gabriel and let the two — no, three men — kill Gabriel, he could have Maizie all to himself again. But murder at a motel is bad for business. He learned that from the cat incident. He pushed aside those malicious thoughts and dialed Gabriel's room, hoping like hell Gabriel picked the phone up right away.

"Hello," Gabriel's voice was low and gruff, disguising it.

Gord got straight to the point, "You have company. Now get the hell out of my motel." There was a three second silent pause, then the other end went dead. Gabriel had hung up on him. He looked at the receiver and swore, "You son of a bitch." He slammed down the receiver. "Well screw you. From now on, you're on your own ... asshole!" From where he sat, he watched Dallas open his door to the two gunmen. He noticed that Cash wasn't wearing the black leather coat Gabriel had described. No machete. That only meant one thing — he would be packing a gun instead.

Not wanting Gabriel to be killed in his motel, ruining what little reputation it had, Gord decided to call Maizie's room.

Her voice friendly as always, "Hey, Gord. What's up?"

His words were hard and concise, "Maizie, shut up, just listen. I don't know how much you know about your boyfriend, but he's in a lot of trouble."

"He's not my boyfriend," she corrected.

He snorted at her, "Whatever." He was going to say more about their date but there was no time for such trivial matters. Instead, he huffed away his jealousy, getting back to why he called, "Look, there are two men here to kill him."

"Russians?"

The fact that she knew about the Russians and had still spent time with Gabriel infuriated him. "So, you do know." Even though Gord couldn't see it, she nodded her head 'Yes.' "Good. If you can think of a way to get him out of my motel before they kill him... do it. And do it fast!"

Maizie thought hard for a few seconds forming a simple plan. "I can do it." She hung up the phone hard and headed straight out the door — without telling Gord what her plans were.

Gord got up from his chair and went to the curtain. He calmly pulled the material back and retrieved the loaded Winchester. He returned to his chair and waited for everything to play out. He kept his eyes on Dallas's door. If they came out shooting, they would have to deal with him. Gord had four rapid shots to end it all right there and then.

~

Gabriel grabbed all the envelopes off the bed and stuffed them into his backpack. Panic was overriding his logic. Should he take the letters with him or hide for Maizie to find? If he took them with him and was killed, they would find them and destroy them. If he left them in the box spring covering, they may still find them if they tossed the room. Either way, they may get their hands on them, so he took his chances, slipping the backpack over his one shoulder. He was standing in the bathtub opening the tiny window above it when he heard a familiar knock.

She had both hands flat on the door, her cheek against it. She called through the metal, loud enough for him to hear, but soft so no one else could, "It's me Maizie. Open up."

He stepped out of the tub and ran to the door to unlock it. As before, hiding behind it, keeping well out of sight of the Russian's room.

Maizie shoved her laundry cart into the room and slammed the door behind her, flipping the deadbolt for safety.

"What are you doing here?" Gabriel furiously demanded.

"I've come to save you."

The suggestion that little Maizie was going to save him from the Russians made him laugh out loud, "And how do you think you're going to do that?"

She flipped open the top of the dirty linen section. "Get in," she ordered.   A very smug self-satisfied grin slipped across her lips.

He half-hugged her one shoulder, "You're brilliant!" Her face flushed hot with the body contact between them. He put one leg over and climbed in, squatting down as small as he could, the backpack hugged tightly against his chest. No sooner had he landed than she laid the sheet from his bed on top of him, covering every inch of his head.

"Ready?"

"Go!"

She walked to the front of the cart and unlocked the door. Holding it open with her elbow, she tugged the cart outside. She called into the room, "See you tomorrow then," pretending she was talking to Gabriel still inside. She let the door casually close behind her. She started down the sidewalk, pretending she was heading towards the laundry room. The cart was much heavier with Gabriel inside it, making it harder for Maizie to maneuver. She had to shove it with all her strength to get it to move straight. Not twist to one side. But slowly she was getting closer to their goal.

~

Inside his room, Dallas was only half-listening to Rene and Cash make their plans. He was more interested in what the housekeeper was doing outside.

Cash turned to Dallas, "So none of the rooms have back doors?" When Dallas didn't answer him, he yelled at him, "Hey stupid ... you listening to me?"

Dallas swatted air at him. "No, I'm not. I'm watching her." He pointed out the window, "Why was she there at his room again? She was already there this morning." Maizie was at the corner of the sidewalk, trying to get the heavy cart to turn to the left. "And why is she having trouble with it. Look at her. She's not pushing it ... she's shoving it."

Rene was annoyed that Dallas was watching women while they were supposed to be making plans, "Who cares about the maid? Are you sure it's him in that room? Are you sure you have the right Gabriel?"

Dallas snorted, "How many guys in this part of Northern Ontario do you think are named Gabriel?"

Cash protested, "So that's what you're basing this on?" He leaned back and threw his hands in the air, "We drove three-hundred miles so we could walk in on an innocent guy we don't want?"

Dallas insisted, "Or it could be him. Only one way to find out, right?" Dallas saw the housekeeper stop in front of the old man's room. He had been standing in his doorway, waiting for her to pass by. Something was bothering Dallas about the whole scene.

Cash stood up, "Let me piss first. Then we'll go get the little prick." Rene groaned that his partner had to go to the bathroom — again.

Dallas continued to watch the housekeeper and the old man, his gut telling him something wasn't right.

~

"Hey, Maizie. What are you doing?" Moses asked from his doorway.

Maizie stopped the cart and acted as casual as she could, "Nothing. Why?" Her breath was labored. Huffing as though she had been doing something strenuous.

"Because your nothing's knee is protruding out the side of your cart." He made a point of not looking down.

Gabriel slowly pulled his knee inward to remove the weight off the tiny rip.

Maizie carefully looked down with only her eyes, keeping her head still. A small rip in the old canvas had started. She also knew from experience that it would rip fast and completely to the edges once it reached a certain length. "Shit," she cursed under her breath. Feeling as though she had no choice, she looked Moses in the eye and explained. "There are men here to kill Gabriel. I'm trying to get him to the laundry room unseen."

"Kill him?" With his decision made in a split second, Moses stepped out of his room, "I can help with that. If they come out, I'll distract them. Nothing slows a person down like a talkative old goat." He took one side of the cart, "Now push."

Not given a choice, she pushed to match his. "Are you sure Moses? It could get dangerous."

He remained looking forward, avoiding her eyes. He didn't want her pity. He said it with dignity. "Maizie ... it's cancer. What could anyone do that could hurt me more."

Maizie's heart sank. "Oh, Moses. I'm so sorry. I didn't realize."

He shrugged, "Let's just get this done." He let go of the cart when it started rolling easy enough for Maizie to control. "Keep going. Save the man."

~

When the old man let go, Dallas finally saw it. "She's got Gabriel in the cart." He jabbed his finger, "Look!"

Rene went to the window and watched as Maizie continued to push the cart at arm's length, throwing her back into it. "Shit!"

Cash reappeared from the bathroom, his gun already drawn. "Let's go!"

All three left Dallas's room at once. All three with their weapons drawn but down, heading for Maizie who was shoving the cart through the laundry room doorway with all her might.

"Good-mornin' gentleman. Beautiful day, isn't it?" Moses greeted from the sidewalk in front of them.

"Get out of the way old man," warned Cash.

He held his hand up to his ear, "What did you say son? I don't hear so good."

~

At his desk, Gord sat up straight when he saw the trio of Russians come out of Dallas's room. Cash leading the way, the other two flanking him two steps behind. Then when old Moses started talking at them, he got to his feet and ordered under his breath "Moses, get out of there. God damned old fool."

He held his breath and aimed his scope right at the side of Dallas's head. He could feel his adrenaline pumping blood through the veins in his neck. All he could do was wait to see if they would harm the old man or just walk around him. His face red and heated, Gord was sure of one thing — if they touched a single hair on Moses's head, they would be dead where they stood.

~

Closer still, Cash growled, "Get out of the way old man. I don't want to hurt you."

Moses pretended to pull back with surprise, "Hurt me, why would you want to hurt me?" He frowned at Cash, crooking his finger at him. "Wait. Don't I know you? Aren't you the Burnett's boy?"

Cash slowed down some but kept on walking his way. He heard Rene curse, "Jesus, just what we needed."

Dallas, not being as cold-blooded as the other two, was hoping for no collateral killings. Especially an old man without a gun to defend himself. He called over Cash's shoulder, "Go back to your room old man. This doesn't concern you."

Moses stayed where he was, pretending to be hard of hearing.

~

Hearing voices out in the courtyard, Tula made her way to the window and watched the commotion. "Figures that dumb ass Moses would be involved," she muttered to herself. She leaned against the window frame for support, stopping herself from going off balance and falling over.

~

Maizie locked the laundry door behind her while Gabriel climbed out of the cart. He stood frozen, thinking for a moment what he should do with his letters. He held out the backpack with one hand, "Maizie, do you have a place in here where you can hide this. I don't want them to find it."

She thought for only a split second, "Yes. In there."

She went to take it from him, but he held onto the strap. His expression was sorrowful, his question earnest, "If I don't make it back, promise me you'll mail them for me."

"I promise," she vowed with a sharp nod. Taking the green backpack from his fisted hand, she understood the importance of the letters it held. "I promise for Heather." She turned around and knelt before the closet marked 'Linens.' She took all the bedding off the bottom shelf and placed it on the floor. She pressed on the one corner of the bottom board and grabbed the opposite edge that stuck upward. She pulled the board up and stuffed the backpack into its hole. She put the board back in place and shoved the bedding back on top of it. She closed the closet again and pulled a box of toilet paper rolls in front of it. She turned around to see him still standing where he was, watching her. She ignored her breaking heart and pointed to the back door. "Go! Out there. Hurry."

Gabriel ran to it, flipped the deadbolt and opened the door. He was about to step out into the cold when he stopped himself. He turned around and went to where Maizie stood. He put his arms around her waist and drew her into him. He kissed her long and hard. When her knees

196

gave way, he stepped back and looked deeply into her eyes. "Thank you, Maizie. I'll never forget you." The shouts from outside pulled them out of their tender moment. Gabriel turned on his heels and left out the back door, heading for his car parked behind the motel.

Maizie's heart crushed in her chest.

Gabriel was gone.

~

Moses stood as wide as he could, blocking the sidewalk. His feet wide apart and his hands placed on his hips so his elbows took up extra space. "Mildred's nephew?"

"GET OUT OF THE WAY!" bellowed Cash.

They were almost on top of Moses yet he refused to move. 'I'm gonna die a hero. Fuck you cancer!' he jeered in his head. He even imagined his hand giving it the finger. This was what he was waiting for. A quick exit from his pain, rather than months of endless agony. Moses grinned widely at him, "Surely you have time to talk to an old friend of your Aunt?"

Without hesitation, Cash raised his gun and shot the old man right in the forehead.

Moses's body jerked backward with the force of the shot. He landed hard, blood spreading from the wound inflicted by the simple pull of Cash's trigger.

Cash stepped over his dead body like it was a bag of garbage and ran for the door they saw Maizie go through. The others did the same. At the laundry room, Cash kicked the door in with his heavy black boot. The other two men waited outside, guns drawn, while Cash searched the laundry room for Gabriel. Not finding him, Cash grabbed Maizie around the waist, holding her in front of him as both a hostage and a shield. He yelled across the courtyard, "WE GOT YOUR GIRLFRIEND, GABRIEL. YOU BETTER COME OUT OR I'LL KILL HER LIKE I DID THE FIRST ONE!"

~

Tula's heart ripped open when she saw Moses drop to the ground. Within seconds her pain turned to anger. "Bastard!" She left the window and stomped straight to her knitting basket. Balls of yarn flew in all directions. From the bottom of it, Tula pulled out a box of ammo along with the 70th birthday gift from her late husband — a Glock with her name engraved on the handle. She needed to put in the bullets. On top of her bed, Tula carefully loaded the pistol even though it was hard to do with her arthritic fingers.

~

Gord, seeing Moses dead on the ground and Maizie being held hostage, aimed his rifle at Cash's head. But Maizie's own head was too close to Cash's to get a clean shot. Gord didn't dare take it, in case he accidentally killed Maizie. Instead, he went for the others. He aimed at Dallas's head and pulled the trigger.

SMASH! The window's glass blew out as the bullet shot through its center, connecting with Dallas's skull a half-second later. Bits of flesh flew in Maizie's direction, landing on her face and arms. Even before Dallas hit the ground, Gord aimed for Rene's back, right behind the heart, and pulled the trigger again. The second man fell to the ground, landing face down. Maizie screamed and flung herself forward with horror, giving Gord the opening he needed. Gord aimed at Cash one more time, lining the Russian's head up in the scope. He held his breath and pulled the trigger. CLICK. Nothing happened. He pulled the trigger again, CLICK. The bullets had jammed in the clip. Gord threw the rifle to the floor and headed to his room for another rifle.

~

In order for Gabriel to escape, he had to drive by the front of the motel. He took one last glance over his shoulder into the courtyard. There, he saw the one situation he feared might happen. Cash had Maizie hostage.

He slammed on the brakes and threw the car into reverse. Without thought for himself, he squealed into the courtyard, honking his horn to get Cash's attention. He flung open the car door, his hands surrendered in the air, "Let her go. She had nothing to do with this. It's me you want. Let her go ... take me instead."

Cash jammed the nose of the gun in Maizie's cheek. "So ... you come here ... and I'll set her free."

What Gabriel saw in the corner of his eye, shocked him. Old Tula was walking towards Cash and Maizie, her arms outward with a big black pistol pointed straight at Cash.

Fully loaded and ready to seek revenge for her lover's murder. Tula lined up Cash's face in the Glock's sights and yelled, "DROP THE GIRL."

When Cash turned to see who was yelling, Maizie's body tilted forward, giving Tula the angle, she wanted. With Maizie's head out of the way, she lined the crosshairs up with his left temple and pulled the trigger. "DIE MOTHER FUCKER!" The kickback from the Glock knocked her frail body on her ass. The bullet pierced the side of Cash's head, blowing half his face off. His body twisted to the ground, releasing Maizie from his hold. In horror, Maizie ran to the nearest wall and clung to it for support.

With all three gunmen shot, Gabriel raced to Maizie's side to comfort her in his arms. He kissed the top of her head, holding her cheek close to his chest. "Oh, Maizie ... I never meant for you to get hurt." Hearing his heart beat wildly in his chest, she burst into tears, sobbing uncontrollably. All he could do was hold her close and make her feel protected. "It's over, Maizie. It'll be safe now."

Down on the sidewalk, Rene's eyes fluttered slightly — he was not completely dead. Through his bloodied eyes, he could see his handgun. He had come to kill Gabriel Carr and that's what he was going to do. He gathered all his strength to complete his final mission.

His trembling hand reached out for his gun and grabbed the handle. He rolled over to face Gabriel and sat up. In one swift move, he aimed his gun and fired one bullet into the side of Gabriel's forehead. He aimed it on

Maizie's face — but before he could get in his kill shot, he felt the sting of two bullets penetrate his own skull. He collapsed to the ground in a heap.

Only after her two bullets made his body jerk and fall to the ground, did she believe that the gunman was definitely dead. That's when Tula lowered her Glock limply to her side. She shuffled her depleted body to where Moses lay dead, his blood pooled dark red on the cement by his body. Standing over him for a moment, she finally dropped to her knees and wept over his body, her gun still clenched in her hand. Her other hand was intertwined with Moses's hand. She wept for the man she loved dearly and who was taken from her forever.

Maizie was hysterical by the time Gord arrived, his rifle clenched in his fist. She was still screaming through her fingers over Gabriel's dead body when he tenderly pulled her close and held her while she sobbed.

They slid down the wall to the cold sidewalk. He sat next to her, his arm around her for comfort. She was trembling, tears streaming down her blood smeared face. He knew there were no words that could ease her terror at witnessing the carnage in front of her. He only held her tight, while trying to control his own emotions about the bloodbath that had happened moments earlier.

~

Within minutes, three OPP cruisers raced into the courtyard, sirens blaring and lights flashing blue and red.

Doors open, guns drawn. But by then, it was all over. They were too late to save anyone. The bloody battle was finished without them.

Even in her state of hysteria over the murders, Maizie said nothing of the backpack hid in the laundry room. Later, during her interrogation, she would only tell the police what she thought they needed to know, leaving the details about the letters out of her statement. Like Gabriel, she was unsure who she could trust — and who she couldn't. And the one man she trusted most, had died holding her in his arms.

EPILOGUE

Gord walked beside Maizie, his hand holding hers. Over her other arm was slung Gabriel's green backpack. The early spring air was fresh and clean. The sun was warm and soothing on Maizie's shoulders — shoulders that carried the weight of the world on them.

It was a short walk from the motel to the downtown core, but each step seemed heavy for Maizie. They stopped in front of the Wawa Post Office, Gord opening the mouth of the exterior mailbox. He saw tears form in Maizie's eyes as she unzipped the backpack.

He comforted her by rubbing up and down her back, "Oh, Maizie. We can do this another day if you want. Another week or two won't matter much."

She sniffed and swallowed down the lump in her throat. "No, it does matter. I've waited too long already." She gathered all the letters in her hand. Not needing the backpack any longer, she let it fall to the ground. "It mattered to Heather. It mattered to Gabriel." She shook them at him with determination, "They died for these."

He rubbed her back again. "It's okay, Maizie. I understand."

"But most of all ...," she wiped away tears from her cheeks, "... it matters to those girls being used as prostitutes at the mall." She held the letters over the opening and let them fall inside. One by one they disappeared into the darkness of the mailbox. When the last one left her fingers, she turned and walked away, sobbing softly at the memory of those who had been murdered for the information the letters held.

Gord let the chute close, then pulled it open again, making sure every letter was inside, starting their journey in bringing justice for Moses, Heather and Gabriel's death. He turned away and ran to catch up with Maizie.

His arm around her, her body leaning on him, they made their way back to their new motel.

After Gord closed down and sold 'The Last Motel', Maizie moved south with him to Wawa, opening their new business together— one that was managed by Gord but designed by Maizie.

Tula being their first guest.

Be sure
to look for
Kay's previous book,
Life on the Lawn

This is the story of four, lifelong, best friends - Fran, Pearl, Ruby and Violet, who attend the auction of Henry Phillips, the husband of their late-friend, Virginia. Henry, no longer able to take care of himself, he is forced to leave the farm life behind and retire into a nursing home. With his unwanted transition, comes the selling of his remaining possessions in a simple country action. Treasures and heirlooms that his greedy children do not care to inherit.

As the sale proceeds, these elderly Southern ladies share with each other the memories and adventures that are connected to many of the items up for auction. Tales of apple pies, lost lovers, and murder. Many of the local folk and neighbours gather to bid on the household items at hand, but it's Emmett, the worldly auctioneer, who is downright curious about the quiet outsider. Why is someone as sophisticated as him at a small town auction? Who is this unknown wealthy Frenchman? And why is he watching the four ladies so intently?

This is the story of one simple day,
at a not so simple auction.

From the author of *Life on the Lawn*

First Page
Last Page

KAY D
JOHNSON

Nitra Zupan faces the one crisis all writers' fear most, losing their entire hand written manuscript weeks before a looming deadline. Worse, she is unable to recapture the essences of her first page, the one she considers to be the most significant page of the entire book. After losing her manuscript to Mother Nature's wrath, she places an ad in the local newspaper offering a reward to have her pages returned to her.

Follow their tense adventure as they encounter the assortment of people who return the pages of her work, only to find them all, except for one. Neither, Nitra nor her house keeper, Wallace McPhee, is aware that the other has feelings that run deeper than their employer, employee relationship. That is, until they encounter the mysterious woman wearing gaudy red lipstick.

The comedic banter between Nitra and Wallace, along with the fast paced adventure, will bring you to the dramatic end of their search for Nitra's first page, the last page.

MARKED

KAY D
JOHNSON

Be sure to
look for
Kay's previous book
MARKED
now on sale.

George Oscar Dack, a white warlock, is on the verge of shaking up his dull, predictable life. With the help of his sarcastic cat, Darius and a strange old woman, he conducts his experiment using precise elements and implements, to cast a spell upon a Canadian two dollar bill.

Writing his initials across the bill's front as part of the spell, it allows him to observe the bill's travels throughout the day, revealing what effects, either good or corrupt, it has on those who possess it, both young and old characters alike. Some have happy encounters, while others definitely do not.

Come join George and follow the bill's many adventures through his ordinary little town and discover the true connection between him and the old woman who enters into his life.

With a new job and a new life,
middle-aged Izzy Abbott finds herself
lonely and terribly bored.

Each evening, to spice up her life,
she disguises herself in an entirely new identity and visits a different
bar, looking for fun, men, and her version of a dirty dry martini
— her perfect martini.

Even though she is having a blast
on her nightly outings, the recent unsolved murder of a woman in the
city lingers in her mind while she party's. Should she feel secure or
watch out for her safety with a killer on the loose?

Meet the quirky patrons and peculiar bartenders she encounters in
the eclectic drinking establishments she visits.

Come join Izzy in
her zany adventures ... in the hunt for
... the perfect martini.

KAY D JOHNSON

Bits
of
Blue

**Be sure
to look for
Kay's previous book
Bits Of Blue**

During a marital dispute between tormented Tess and her abusive husband, she finally gathers the courage to fight back for the first time. The result is the unintentional death of Morty Logan. Although it was an accident, Tess was convinced she would be blamed for his gruesome death if she called the authorities.

Determined to stay out of prison for the crime she did not commit, Tess hatched a plan to get rid of the dead body before the summer's heat wave gave her away.

Follow her internal struggles as she disposes of the body, bit by bit, using the one item she had plenty of — little blue zip bags, a sale item her controlling husband demanded she buy by the case.

While doing so, she must hide her true missions from the very nosy neighborhood senior and his friend, the meddlesome cop, both suspiciously watching every move she made.

No one knew what the timid Tess Logan had inside her tote bag as she walked about the city, looking for new places to leave her Bits of Blue

Be sure
to look for
KAY'S
previous book

An Angel Named Topaz

In the winter of 1977, Mickey Backus hires a Private Investigator to follow his wife Rosie, who he suspects is cheating on him. Not only did he want proof of the affair, he was also curious as to who was dumb enough to fool around with the wife of Belleville's notorious mobster. Thank goodness, Mickey still had his beloved blue lined angel fish to talk to.

When Bernie, Mickey's right-hand man, also hires a Private Investigator, the competition heats up with everyone trying to get the photos the mobster wants. But when all is revealed by the Private Investigators, the identity of Rosie's lover both shocks and angers Mickey, setting off a chain of unexpected events that no one could have predicted, especially those of hookers and murder.

Come follow the bizarre string of episodes that entangle the even odder cast of characters — one being — **An Angel Named Topaz.**

Lovage

When single mom, Charlotte Thomas, moved into her new house,
she had no idea that the man living across the street would take
such offense to her scraping all the grass off her yard with a
bulldozer. Against his friendly advice, she was determined to
landscape her yard the way she wanted, no matter how much the
good-looking Jack Lawson protested. Out came the grass — In
went the stone, pea gravel and an abundance of vegetation, finally
giving her lovage plant a permanent home.

But it was the elderly lady next door, along with her teenaged
daughter, that quickly became very persistent matchmakers. Nicky
and dear old Dottie were convinced that her mother needed a man
to help Charlie create the garden of her dreams. A man that would
eventually fall head over heels for the natural beauty
of the stubborn blonde.

Come follow the romantic adventure of Charlotte and her
neighbours, as they landscape her little wartime home.
Who knows, you might learn some
new gardening techniques along the way.